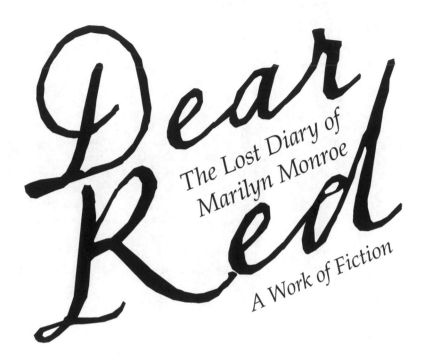

Dear Red

The Lost Diary of Marilyn Monroe

A Work of Fiction

Maureen McNeil

ARCHWAY
PUBLISHING

Archway Publishing books may be ordered through booksellers or by contacting:

Archway Publishing
1663 Liberty Drive
Bloomington, IN 47403
www.archwaypublishing.com
1 (888) 242-5904

ISBN: 978-1-4808-5377-5 (sc)
ISBN: 978-1-4808-5376-8 (e)

Library of Congress Control Number: 2017916510

Print information available on the last page.

Archway Publishing rev. date: 11/02/2017

For Paul

Author's Preface

More than fifty years since Marilyn Monroe's death, one is still struck by her image on the streets of New York: her wink from a dusty poster in the window of a Chinese laundry; her face tattooed on the brown shoulder of a young Latina; the red velvet nude adorning a tote in the subway; her gray-blue eyes staring from the cover of *Vanity Fair*. Yet each time we worship the sex goddess, we overlook the painful bullying to which she was subjected during her deification.

Marilyn was an unconventional, vivid, playful, and driven actor who sometimes collaborated with the media and the Hollywood studios that sold her as orphaned, tragic, and miserable. The story behind these images raises many troubling questions. Why do we victimize those who liberate us from our own hidebound thinking? Why do we wait for sexually radiant women to get their comeuppance? And why is the narrative of female helplessness still appealing to both men and women today?

Marilyn's death from barbiturate overdose in interaction with other drugs was never investigated. The death of the woman who had just days before negotiated a million-dollar contract with Twentieth Century Fox, who was in the midst of setting up her long-dreamed of Shakespearean company, was, in the popular imagination at least, summarily ruled a suicide. As an act of social justice, I've taken it upon myself to explore Marilyn's emotional life during her last seven months. Despite her omnipresence, I felt Marilyn was long-lost—that she might be found if given the same chance for mundane expression the living enjoy. Sticking to historical facts and when necessary, conjectures of poetic and thematic truth, the diary format gave me the chance to discover more of her identity each day.

Alongside the iconic images we all love, I present a less-airbrushed portrait. Her face is freckled, and her legs bloodied from her menstrual cycle. Her body requires toning through yoga, weight lifting, hula hoops, and bras worn at night. I imagine a glimpse of her library, her poetry, her insomniac nights, her "communist" trip to Mexico, her animal studies at the zoo, escapades with Brando, and the silly stenographer outfit she wore as a disguise on her dates with Dreamboat.

Marilyn could have settled into the privileged life of the movie star. Instead she devoted herself to making art. She thought her talent, captured on celluloid, would surely gain the respect that paternalistic American attitudes of the times had begrudged her. She believed it would one day erase her image of being a dumb, scandalous, and mentally unbalanced blond. Her acting coach, Lee Strasberg, often touted the adage that art is longer than life. I'm not sure this has been the case with Marilyn. The distortions of celebrity seem to have won out thus far. While I leave the task of assessing her films to others who are more qualified, I am gratified to offer here another take on Marilyn.

The most poetical topic in the world is the death of a beautiful woman.

—E. A. Poe

SUNDAY, JANUARY 1, 1962

Dear Red,

I'm going to write daily observations of my hope, dreams, and fears so one day someone will read it and know Marilyn was a real human bean. Norma Jeane, Norma Jeane, the human bean! That's what the kids at school used to say.

I've decided to call you Red—the color of your soft-bound leather by Hermes. I love your thick, creamy paper on the inside too. I picked you out while I was Christmas shopping. A gift for me—why not? Oh, I've tried to write about my life and failed, but this time it's real because I'm writing alone—by myself. All I've ever written are shopping lists, little poems, notebooks on acting, and facts to remember for conversation with important people. My goal this time is to write every day and trust that whatever it turns out to be, it will be *me*.

Gee, I've spent my life reading scripts, saying lines into a mirror, and charming the press, and yet, when I write my thoughts down on paper, I don't even recognize them. I scratch out what I write, then realize afterward—wait a minute—I said what I meant! So no chicken scratch allowed. Maybe one day this diary will give some kid the courage to dream big.

I've had a hard time lately talking to Dr. G. When I told him I was writing a diary, he said, "Good! Writing is like an enema—it'll clean you out. And you can read your diary out loud to me." *Fuck that*, I said to myself. Geminis are private.

A few unnamed friends suggested that I keep a diary to cover my posterior. "Marilyn," they tell me, "it's not your butt, it's your back you've got to watch!" I know I've got enemies. People say terrible things about me. Lies. I always say, "Consider the source."

"Forgive your enemies, just never forget who they are," Dreamboat said. I said to him, "I see them every day, so how could I forget their names?"

January 2, 1962

Dear Red,

Did I mention my New Year's resolution? Marry Dreamboat and knock *Cleopatra* off the front page of *Life Magazine*. I've given up eating mammals too. Steak is my favorite food, and it doesn't make me fat, but I feel guilty eating it. After all, cows are mammals like me.

Every year I cross off one of my favorite foods. Last year it was peanut butter and jelly sandwiches on white bread with no crust. The year before I gave up eating Twinkies. Oh, I'm no angel, if that's what you think I'm saying. But gee, I can at least try to be what I say I am. If I don't like hurting animals, how can I eat them? I still eat birds even though I love my parakeets Bobo and Butch—but Arthur got them in the settlement. I know that doesn't make sense. And I eat tuna from a can, shrimp cocktail, baked salmon. I'm not thinking of going totally vegetarian yet, even though some people say vegetarianism could save the world.

Breakfast: two oranges, squeezed, black coffee
Lunch: one boiled egg, salt, four celery stalks, black coffee
Dinner: peas and carrots mixed, grilled chicken, bubbly

January 3, 1962

Dear Red,

Oy vey! Paula, my coach for *Something's Got to Give*, called. She paraphrased my annual astrology update: "Marilyn, you're going to make a lot of money!"

"Fuck money," I said. "All I care about is love!" People think I'm crazy, but when you learn to be yourself, you get used to disappointing others.

"Paula," I said, "do you think I'm too busted up about Arthur for romance?"

"No, Marilyn, I don't mean that. It's just that you want to be taken seriously."

"Could you send me a copy of the horoscope?" I asked.

I hoped she wasn't thinking of asking for another raise. Between me and Fox, she is getting five thousand a week as my coach. I mean, I used to live on five dollars a week.

"Paula," I said, "I'm nobody's fool. I don't borrow. I know how to steal and make it my own."

What is truly amazing is that Dreamboat and I feel like equals when we are alone, yet right now, he is in charge of world peace and keeping the H-bomb from getting into the wrong hands while I spend the day reciting lines and looking at myself in the mirror!

I put on Ella Fitzgerald to exercise.
Dumbbells, twenty minutes.
Floor exercises, twenty minutes.

I switched to a stack of Frank Sinatra records.
Hula hoop, twenty minutes.
Chin exercises.

JANUARY 4, 1962

Dear Red,

I wasn't abandoned. Mother paid for me to be taken care of when I was twelve days old. She was single and had to work! When I was older,

Mother, Aunt Grace, or Aunt Ana took me to the movies every Sunday. They planted the seed in me about becoming the next Jean Harlow. We all dreamed out loud together.

Last time I tried to write about me, it sounded like Ben Hecht, and we never finished the project. So this is my chance. I don't care if it jumps, skips, or stutters in bits and pieces. That's what I want—the truth. The whole truth. *Me*. Nothing but *me*. I mean, lying is okay sometimes. I tell lies, but I appreciate the truth. The truth is deeper than honesty, says Lee.

Sister Aimee Semple McPherson, the Hollywood preacher, taught mother to dream. She believed in divorced women, single moms, poor Mexicans, and Negros and that everyone needed to dance and sing and have a second chance in life.

Bad, bad news. Darryl Zanuck is back as president of Twentieth Century Fox after being fired a few years ago. He is the one who typecast me as the blond bombshell, like I'm nothing but a character actor or personality, and now he thinks he's going to use me to save his company's ass. That really hits a girl where it hurts. Well, my schtupping days are over. Wait until he sees who is in charge. I owe them one more picture—to be jointly produced with Marilyn Monroe Productions—and a director and writer on my approval list. Other low blows in life:
   + Mother's spells
   + my dog Tippy shot dead when I was nine
   + Johnny Hyde's death in 1950
   + miscarriages
   + Grace's suicide
   + gallbladder surgery
   + Payne Whitney Clinic
   + Pauline Kael's reviews

Wow, I'm really depressing myself. I better list the good stuff:
   + dates at the Carlyle Hotel
   + Dom Perignon, 1953

- Actors' Studio
- Whitey's makeup
- the Korea performance
- making Matzo ball soup for Arthur
- Tom Kelley's nude
- Fred Karger teaching me to sing
- Rafe's late-night massages

Hairdressers always hear the buzz first, so if you want to know the news, make an appointment!

Tomorrow I have to take down my Christmas tree. Needles are all over my apartment, and they hurt my feet! The tree is still pretty, though. And I'm sentimental because Joe and I decorated it on Christmas Eve. We took a special trip to Olivera Street to buy Mexican ornaments. I made one of his mother's homemade pasta recipes minus the garlic and olives and all the things Joe doesn't like, and we toasted bubbly and exchanged gifts. I gave him a photograph of us from our honeymoon in Japan as we got off the plane. Someone sent it to me. And I gave him a jar of blackberry jam I made last summer when I was recuperating from gallbladder surgery. I picked the berries with my friend Anne Karger. She nursed me for a week. Joe is very sweet too since our divorce, especially rescuing me from Dr. Kris last year when she "accidentally" had me locked up in the psychiatric ward. I'll always be grateful to Joe for getting me out of there. He gave me a long yellow silk nightgown and some black lingerie for Christmas. I don't wear either, and he knows it. And he gave me a big bottle of Chanel No. 5. This morning I counted sixty-five bottles! Joe must have given me at least a dozen.

January 5, 1962

Dear Red,

I've never owned anything besides a dress, a pair of shoes, a piano, and a car, but Dr. G and his friend Eunice Murphy are trying to convince me to buy a house. I want to live in New York, but I fell in love with a Spanish-style bungalow in Brentwood for $90,000. Latin above the door read *cursum perficio*—my destiny.

Gee, the house is sweet! I'd like to own a home with a husband, but on the other hand, who wants to wait? Dreamboat and I can't marry for seven years from now, when he's done with politics. And every actress needs a place of her own in LA if she wants to make a living in the movies—even if New York is really home. Maybe I'll call up that handsome poet I met New Year's Eve—Jose Bolanos. He invited me to Mexico. I could ask Mrs. Murray to come along on a shopping spree to help me buy furniture for the house. She helped Dr. G furnish his. I just love blue Mexican tiles, terra cotta bowls, and woven blankets. I'd like a big, heavy, family-size dining room table. Yes, I said. Yes, I will. Yes. Just like Molly Bloom. Yes, is my new favorite word. I want to buy this house.

I have two beautiful girlfriends named Pat in my life, and I love them both—Pat Lawford, Dreamboat's sister married to Peter, and Pat Newcomb, my publicist. Just so we don't get mixed up, I'll call Pat Newcomb "Pat," and I'll call Pat Lawford "Pat Lawford." I spend a lot of time with Pat, my publicist. She's really my closest friend. I know you could argue she can't be both because she's not a friend if I pay her, but she is! She's smart, and she believes in me. She's a cutie-pie with good taste buds. And she keeps her mouth shut. She listens. She really cares. And did I say she's funny? And the thing I love most about Pat is she's a single working girl like me, and she's smart about men.

Breakfast: yucky health drink, black coffee
Lunch: yogurt mixed with strawberry preserves, black coffee
Dinner: tuna, onions, capers, crackers, bubbly

Dear Red,

I found out this afternoon my friend David Brown was fired from *Something's Got to Give!* He's been replaced by Henry Weinstein—someone Dr. G knows. Isn't that strange? And my director, Cukor, is furious. Not good. This film is already in trouble.

"Paula, when are you planning to fly to LA?" I asked.

She said she is still recovering from the scorching of *The Misfits*—her black drapery and black scarf under a black umbrella in hundred-degree heat! I give my friends nicknames. Paula is Black Bart, and I call myself Zelda Zonk, but the crew calls Paula the Black Mushroom and worse. They blamed her *and* me when really nearly everyone on the damn set of *Misfits* had their own private meltdown. I'm afraid I'm seen as a wimp or a fool because I don't fight. I can look out at the big Pacific Ocean and see that the world doesn't revolve around me. I'm a pacifist.

"Does she or doesn't she?" It's a new TV ad about hair color.

I read about a suicide in the newspaper today, and I wondered what the story was. It's a touchy subject and an easy coverup. Rather than getting messy, people accept, "Oh, she was sick" or "She was crazy" or "It was meant to be." I'm no fool. Gee, I get angry thinking about the manipulation that would follow, discounting my whole career—if—if I accidentally took too much medication. I'm careful with pills.

My neighbor, Jeanne Carman, popped over tonight with bubbly to toast the New Year. I met her five years ago at the Actors Studio. She seemed kind of lonely. She invited me to play golf. She'll teach me. She says she's kind of a trickster. Wolves "hi-baby" her, too. She wanted to know my makeup techniques. I told her to think of makeup like clothes—you wear it or you don't. You don't do it half way. So I made up her face and then

I told her I had someplace I had to go. It was sunset, so I went running toward the Santa Monica beach. It's only a couple miles from my Doheny apartment.

JANUARY 7, 1962

Dear Red,

I met Dreamboat at a fundraiser in 1951. Peter Lawford invited me. We both fell in love that night—me with the senator and he with the senator's sister. He said, "I read that you could fetch the wolves out of any jungle, asphalt or otherwise."

I asked, "Do you really read the film reviews?"

He said, "I do." But our eyes said much more.

I'm reading Willy Shakespeare, trying not to pay attention to Maf, my little pooch, laying flat on his belly, his hind legs stretched out behind him, his front paws holding my foot as he licks my toes. I scream out loud even though it's 3:30 in the morning and I really, really, really, really want to sleep.

Inez stopped by for lunch and said Mother is fine. I am grateful for her news. Unfortunately, mother is a Christian Scientist, and her religion doesn't allow her to take medication that would help her. I dream of her being able to live near me—not in the sanitarium—but she is delicate and unpredictable, nothing I can handle unless she takes her medication.

It's 3:39. I've called everyone I can think of. I've taken pills. I've drunk champagne. I've sung my favorite Sinatra, soaked in the bath, and done the insomnia exercises Carl Sandburg gave me. I tried Freud's free association.

Today Dr. G and I went back and forth saying the first word that came into our minds. Then I had to do it myself. It was like counting sheep: Maf. Frankie. Cal Neva. Blood. Endometriosis. Mother. Daddy Miller. Clark Gable. Misfits. Barbiturates. Sydney. Shit, I'm hungry. I can't eat. I've got that little pad of fat under my chin that is making me crazy. I tied a kerchief around my head to help it stay in place, but I took it off because I can't sleep.

It's 3:46, 3:48, 3:50. I'm watching the clock tick round and round—3:51. If I had a house, I could garden. I could plant flowers like I used to admire when I was a kid walking to school. It's 3:56. Dinner at the Lawfords' tomorrow.

It's 3:59. I read *The Seven Deadly Sins*, poems with wood engravings by Leonard Baskin. It has line drawings of half monsters, half humans. When I consider envy, I have to admit Elizabeth Taylor comes to mind. Sloth, yes. I adore soaking in Chanel No. 5. Avarice—I don't know what avarice means exactly. I have to look that up. Pride. I couldn't act without pride. It's important for an actress to take pride in her work. Gluttony, yes, for the camera. I crave the camera. Still, the entire world will say *lust* is my vice. They couldn't be more wrong. My sin is accepting human nature. It's 4:13. My sin is being me. My sin is my innocence, of not being ashamed of who I am. It's 4:15. I feel heavy, like a slow pulling of flesh and bone, sinking into the mattress. Maybe writing is the pill.

I'm not a writer, but I know how words affect an audience. I hate the word *obey*. And even though I used it, I don't like the word *hate*. I like the word *courage*—it works like a drug. Dreamboat is writing a book about courage, taking risks, overcoming fear. I like the word *nincompoop* because it's a compound word with a funny sound. I read it in *Madame Bovary*, which of course is translated from French, so it was the translator's choice. They could have used fool. I like that word too because as Willy Shakespeare is so good at pointing out, all humans are foolish. I've learned that when people are mean or foolish, it doesn't help to be bitchy back. I like the words *peace* and *love* and *respect*. I've learned that being alone is better than being used. When your husband has an affair or someone lies to your face, a fight won't make it any better.

I know what love is, and I am loved. Isn't that the first human right?

JANUARY 8, 1962

Dear Red,

Fox's new boy, Henry Weinstein, is keeping tabs on me. Rafe, my massage therapist, said there was a strange car parked outside my driveway. I haven't met Weinstein yet, but he calls every day now to see how I f-e-e-e-e-l. Fox is worried about their investment. Fuck him. Fuck the world.

The Twentieth Century Fox script of *Something's Got to Give* finally arrived—a second-to-the-last shitty script for me. I owe them one last film, my thirtieth, after this. Cukor is directing—he owes one too. He's stuck like me. I called Nunnally Johnson and asked him to please help with the rewrite. He says it'll be easy.

"You're a natural comedian, Marilyn. I can fix it. Just mark an X where it's something you wouldn't say and a double XX where it's not funny."

The Fox lot has turned into a fucking ghost town! I went to wardrobe to borrow a black dress for tonight, and even the cafeteria was closed! Rats were scurrying between the buildings and bushes. *Cleopatra* is running Fox into the ground. I feel so much pressure to help save the studio, but why should I? Why not Liz?

"Call the shots, Marilyn," Dad said on the phone. "You have chutzpah, a nerve like gold."

That's why I love him—people think I'm nuts to call Isidore Miller Dad because he's my ex-father-in-law. But the law doesn't say I had to give up Dad when I divorced Arthur. He's a big supporter.

Pat Lawford called and suggested I get out of bed, bundle up, and meet her in Venice to take a beach walk. I told her I'm not done making my phone calls. Besides, Weinstein would probably follow us.

January 9, 1962

Dear Red,

Lunched with Dean and Jean Martin at Chasen's on Beverly Boulevard. Frankie showed up too. He's been working up at Cal Neva and invited me for the gala opening in June. Frank Sinatra and I have been friends since I was sixteen. My first husband, Jimmy, introduced us one night when we were out dancing with his friend Bob Mitchum. Bob met Jimmy in the army.

After lunch I treated myself at the gallery on la Cienega Boulevard. I'd been eyeing a small bust of lovers by Rodin for a month now. I fell in love with his *Hand of God* at the Met a few years ago. It reminds me of how I feel with Dreamboat, but it makes me a little sad.

If only love had really blinded me like in the Greek myth. If only I didn't see Arthur's diary left open on the table, maybe our marriage could have worked. I didn't mind supporting him—I just minded being his subject and his labeling me and analyzing me like I was a teapot, not his wife or lover. I miss walking arm in arm with Arthur down Fifty-Seventh Street, riding bikes in Sheepshead Bay. But he shut himself up writing for days and weeks without talking to me. He just wrote about me, and that is no fun.

Last night I got mad all over again and gave Maf the white beaver coat Arthur bought for me. I figure someone should enjoy it. He looked beautiful.

Joe suggested on New Year's Eve that we marry again, but I told him his love is old fashioned. My talent is physical, like his. I make walking a whole new ballgame—but he just doesn't get it. He's jealous when guys look at me. Sure, I'd be the happiest woman in the world if I could satisfy him, but he can't allow me the freedom I need to work.

Abraham Lincoln said all men are created equal. He meant *all humans*. Negros, Mexicans, Indians, Chinese, homosexuals, and women and children are equal to white men. I read books about how he stopped a sixteen-state rebellion from tearing the country in half by upholding the Constitution. And he stuck to his goal through psychological spells and sadness. That's why I keep his portrait on my living room mantel. Being smart and driven is lonely.

JANUARY 10, 1962

Dear Red,

I gave Shelly the list of men I want to sleep with. She forgot her list. Now that's not fair! She complained that my list were all dead men, and I said when I eliminated those I'd already slept with, it didn't leave a very interesting bunch. She demanded a new list of the top living men.

I said, "That's easy." There is only one living man I want, so I wrote his name ten times.

Now she wants my top ten women list. Number one is Eleonora Duse. I read that her quivering lip created a volcano. Isn't that something? And her silences were like a roar—and rumor has it that she literally drinks her lovers. And she was funny and just naturally understood sense memory. But Shelly said no dead women. I told her she's not going to get a list of living women from me until she hands over her list of top ten living men.

January 11, 1962

Dear Red,

I've decided on a Swedish accent for Ellen when she pretends she's the nanny. It's a sexy choice. I get a kick out of it. Paula is sending tapes for me to listen to, and she's setting up a date for me to meet with a tutor, a wonderful actress who studied with Lee named Edith Evenson, a tall, luminous brunette, somebody I met at one of Lee's New Year's Eve parties. Paula agrees that Swedish will brighten up *Something's Got to Give*.

It seems like I have three buttons: Live. Sleep. Die. And my live button is stuck on. Know why I can't sleep? Blame the studios who started us out on "vitamin" injections so we could perform endless hours. Dr. Kris said I can rebuild my sleep activator through hypnosis. For now, Dr. E gives me injections. Dr. G gives me pills. I drink Champagne, vodka, gin. All three leave me fucked.

January 12, 1962

Dear Red,

Dad called to ask how things are going. I told him about the beautiful bungalow in Brentwood at the dead end of Helena Drive.

He's always rooting for me. He likes to tell me that Marilyn is Fox's biggest commodity. I said I'm in great form. I'm at home tonight developing my talent in private, like Lee says. I'm reading, bathing, talking on the phone. Plato says the truth lies in between—that's where I am. Between one side and the other. Between innocence and experience. Between sheets. Between legs. Between selves. Between inside and out. Between fact and fiction. Between birth and death. It is called art.

JANUARY 13, 1962

Dear Red,

I remember thinking when I married Jimmy that maybe we could be married without having sex because I was only sixteen and didn't understand what it was all about. No one would tell me. Beebe, my friend, made it sound nasty and painful, and all I really wanted was to play kickball with the kids after dinner. But I was anxious to please him, and it turned out sex is fun and athletic too!

I was always happy when Jimmy was around. We took drives and had picnics at the beach and fished in the mountains. Saturday nights went to Grauman's Chinese Theatre for a dime. I used to go there when I was growing up with Mother. That's where I first saw *Little Women*. But I didn't like it when Jimmy went to work and left me alone, and especially when he went to war—he was so excited. I moved in with his mother, and she got me the job in the Radio Airplane Factory and taught me how to drive a stick. But when David Conover took those photos of me for *Yank* magazine and I started at the Blue Book Modeling Agency, his mother was nervous. I posed in print ads, selling Luster Cream shampoo, Jantzen Swimwear, American Airlines, cigars, suntan lotion, lipstick, diet pills, and hair coloring. I moved in with my mother for a while. We lived above Aunt Ana Lower, Grace Goddard's aunt. Jimmy and I had passionate weekends when he came home on leave, but when he came home for good, I tried to make him understand that my life had taken a new direction. I drove to Nevada and got a divorce.

JANUARY 14, 1962

Dear Red,

Even an atheist Jew like me finds something comforting about saying the Sh'ma. Jews are supposed to say it before dying, or in my case, flying.

I'm nervous, and I have to relax. I'm on my way to New York to work on a private moment—that's a method exercise. I need to buy a whole new casual wardrobe. I've got a hair appointment, and I'll have dinner with Dad. He's flying up from Florida.

Tuesday and Friday I have morning classes at the Actors Studio, like old times. I love working in front of a live audience. Still, I'm not sure how I could ever get the energy to perform on stage night after night, month after month, like Susie did in *The Diary of Anne Frank*. Lee thinks I could do it, but it's more thrilling to make love to a camera than one giant audience.

The moon is perfectly illuminated, bigger than life on the black screen, and its light is pointing at me through the window into my bedroom. It's so bright I can't take my eyes off it. But it's the dark side I worry about, like the dark side of my head. Dr. G sat with a pen in hand today for an hour, and I didn't have a single thought. There was not a cloud in the big blue sky. I couldn't squeeze out even one word. I figure I pay him, so I'd rather listen to him talk about Freud and stream of consciousness than open my mouth. Besides, my eyes just wanted to close. I feel safe on his couch. It's when I try to sleep at night in my bed that a big, lonely cave opens up inside me, and I get all fucked up and squeeze my pillow, trying to turn myself inside out to make my brain stop. I take Dr. G's pills and Dreamboat's pills. I'll try anyone's pills to get to sleep, and still I'm the world's biggest insomniac.

JANUARY 15, 1962

Dear Red,

I'm so depressed. The phone won't ring. Dreamboat won't take my calls. We are supposed to have a date. I know I make his back feel better, and he always shows up eventually, but why doesn't he return my call? I know he's at the Carlyle. I walked by last night in my brown wig and dumpy coat. He should have recognized me with the secretary's notebook he always insists I carry.

I saw a specialist who wants to do a colonoscopy to check out my chronic pain. My gynecologist wants to rule out any colon problems. I'm not sure if I want to go through with it. The procedure sounds horrible. Of course, I'd be knocked out, so I wouldn't feel a thing, but there is this bowel cleaning the day before I'm not keen on. He says it's no worse than an enema.

I love the view of Fifty-Seventh Street from my thirteenth-floor apartment and spending time with the art I've collected over the last decade: a black stone bust of Queen Nefertiti, a beautiful Toulouse-Lautrec, and a large male (of course) nude statue by William Zorach. And in my favorite portrait—a photograph by Cecil Beaton from 1956—I'm wearing the white gown, lying across a white bed, holding a red carnation. The look on my face is inviting, without putting anything on. Eve Arnold once told me that I photograph ten pounds lighter than I am. I told her it's a trick Houdini taught me. She looked amused, like I was telling the truth.

January 16, 1962

Dear Red,

It's the freedom of New York that inspires me. New York is my home. Walking around, I can forget the slavery of Hollywood. Bundled in fur, I am anonymous, or I can be Marilyn, depending how I walk and how much hair is showing. New York reminds me of four mostly good years with Arthur. I'm proud I backed him through the McCarthy witch hunt and that he didn't name names. If the State Department threw anything at him, they threw it at me too, and my fan clubs wouldn't stand to see me beaten.

I still can't get through to Dreamboat at the office or the Carlyle. This has never happened before. It's been a week now I've left messages. I ate and drank like a pig tonight. Lena, my housekeeper, cooked my favorite lasagna with spinach instead of meat. I'm eating instead of the phone ringing. If I get fat, it's his fault.

JANUARY 17, 1962

Dear Red,

Lee says I've got actor's gold—a responsive instrument. Well, he's not the first man to think so. He talks to me on Chekhov and my natural impulses and uses concrete examples so I know exactly what he means. He encourages me not to shut memories out: trust the method. Don't act out of fear. The technique gives you a position of strength.

Paula was making pot roast in the kitchen. She said, "Remember, manure fertilizes roses." I don't really like that old adage.

When I asked Lee how he thinks I could ever get up on stage night after night, he said, "Marilyn, dramatic acting is your talent. You must develop it." His symphony on the record player started skipping, so he ended the conversation. He got up to make the next choice. I guess I've got to be like that. When the time comes, I'll make the decision.

Tomorrow I'm working with him on Ellen's character for *Something's Got to Give,* even though I'd really like to do a scene from *Three Sisters.* Natasha is an awkward girl who is made fun of by two snotty sisters because she's in love with their brother, Andrei. But by the end of the play, she's got all the power.

The Strasberg eight-room apartment overlooks Central Park West. Every room is filled floor to ceiling with tempting books. I moved in between marriages—after Joe and before Arthur. I remember Sunday dinners, smooching with Jimmy Dean. So alive! Alive! He was brilliant. I remember playing Lorna Doone. I sang *I'll Get by as Long as I've Got You* and proved I belonged at the Actors Studio. I passed the test, so to speak, but it was rough. None of the students thought I belonged on stage. Susie was dating Richard Burton. Johnny was rejecting his father—he gave up his bed for me and slept in the living room, so I gave him my sports car when he turned twenty-one. Dr. Kris, my shrink, was downstairs, but it was Lee I craved. He rocked me to sleep when needed a good cry.

JANUARY 18, 1962

Dear Red,

I met up with Warhol at Sardi's. He is usually a dear, listening to my dilemmas, but last night he gave me hell for falling in love with brand-name men. I said, "Look who's talking brand names!" I told him if a girl isn't ahead of her times, she's behind! At his studio on Union Square, he photographed me. "Just your head," he said, "not your behind."

Freddy Karger's sister called. Freddy was my singing tutor I fell in love with in the classic way, head over heels. He was warm, smart, generous, curious, and energetic. He taught me everything, from sex to architecture to geography. As the Columbia Pictures studio vocal coach, he taught me *the* big thing—how to *sing*. By now I've recorded seventeen albums! And not only singing, Freddy taught me how to get rid of the bad vocal habits so I could use my speaking voice as an instrument. He took me to clubs and romantic dinners in Malibu, the Hollywood Bowl concerts, and got me reading and going to museums. Because of Freddy, I signed up for courses at UCLA on art and literature. He oozes confidence and is a stimulating conversationalist.

But Freddy loved Jane Wyman! When I got pregnant, I knew what to do. Everyone knew the phone number of doctors who did abortions back then. We didn't think much about it. Legal or illegal, abortion has been around since Adam and Eve. But every actress I know breathed a sigh of relief when birth control pills became available and we didn't have to worry anymore.

JANUARY 19, 1962

Dear Red,

I got my call. Dreamboat sent a car. I had to wear the dowdy brown secretary outfit, but it was worth it. Champagne, caviar, music. A few dances and we were able to slip into the master suite. We talked about the future of America while we made love, and then he dozed in my arms. I was euphoric. When he left, he said, "Baby, remember, we are all mortal."

Porter bleached my hair pillowcase white. Wonder what Whitey will think. It's like the big moon that shines in my window! He'll have to adjust my makeup now. Blissful shopping at Bloomies, Saks, I. Magnin. Bought pants in black, white, beige, and red, and dresses and a beautiful red leather Gucci bag—something a girl owes herself now and then. I love Emilio Pucci. Really, the sales ladies couldn't have been more shocked when they saw me naked at Bloomingdales. Doesn't the whole world know by now I don't wear a bra or panties? They must not have recognized Marilyn. They were upset to put the dresses back on the rack after I tried them on— as if pubic hair spoiled them—so I bought them all. As I told Lena, shopping is a natural way for a girl to keep her chin up. Her little sons stopped by to say hello. I adore them. They've grown so big and so tall and strong and handsome and smart—and they're only six and eight years old!

JANUARY 20, 1962

Dear Red,

I borrowed a pencil from a handsome actor at the studio, and he took me for a coffee. His name is Geoffrey, just a boy really, the one who blew up the bridge in Sam Spiegel's, *Bridge on the River Kwai*. I asked what people whisper about me. He said they all marvel at my ass in blue jeans, my freckled face with no makeup, and hair wrapped in a head scarf. I revealed some of my beauty secrets, like Vaseline and wax on my cheeks and lips, Nivea moisturizer or lanolin or olive oil and beer in my hair, lemon for my nails, and ice baths with Chanel No. 5. I told him my cobbler cuts one heel a quarter inch shorter than the other to help me walk. When he said I was instinctively smart, I put a dollar on the table and kissed his cheek. I had to get out of there!

PS: It's snowing!

January 21, 1962

Dear Red,

I entertained Norman and Hedda Rosten with my nightmares of Brueghel and Bosch and a whole underworld of devils I saw at the Metropolitan yesterday. Patricia, now eight, wanted to hear the story about the time I rode a pink elephant at Madison Square Garden and threw pixie dust to thousands of fans. That's what she wanted to do when she grows up. I smiled and told Hedda I'm starting a college fund for her.

I didn't dare walk down "our" block of Montague Street—but I did insist that we walk along the promenade to gaze at the great big sparkly diamond of Manhattan. That's what I used to call it when I stood there with Arthur.

On my way home, I walked past the Plaza and carriages to Central Park looking through the trees. The lights in the mist made beautiful rainbows and halos. I walked over the famous subway grate in front of Wright's Food on Lexington too—that's where the publicity stunt of *The Seven Year Itch* was filmed. Of course, that's a bittersweet memory. On the other hand, the ad created a sensation for a so-so movie.

Wow! I wore myself out. I wonder if New Yorkers realize how much exercise they get when they go shopping! I stopped for coffee and doodled on a paper napkin. Gestures—people as they bend, drag, point, slump, sip coffee, basically, indicating how they feel—like me—pooped! I studied people as they walked down the street, too. Most wear a masklike expression. Only once in a while I can tell someone is connecting with his or her inner self. When they do, they look engaged, natural, and curious. Like a monkey!

JANUARY 22, 1962

Dear Red,

Every time I go into Cedars of Lebanon Hospital for corrective GYN surgery, the press calls it an abortion. Pat told me that some journalists claim I've had twelve abortions. Bullshit! The world doesn't really get how two-faced it is. If only women could impregnate themselves, the gossip would stop.

Back in LA, it's Sunday, my day off. I don't comb my hair or wear stockings. No makeup. It's a treat. Dr. G and his family are okay with this. I went to dinner as usual. Joan, Dr. G's daughter, played me a record by a group she's mad about, and she showed me this new dance called the twist. I love dancing with her. I think I lost an inch of fat off my ass!

Dad called, and I told him I'm going to teach him the latest dance. How cute to see a seventy-year-old man doing the twist. He wanted immediate instructions. I suggested that he turn on some loud music with a beat: lift his elbows, twist at the waist, and rock back and forth, lifting one foot at a time, and snap his fingers!

I want to set the record straight. I didn't grow up with *Ozzie and Harriet*, but I was loved. I lived in an orphanage for a year or so. I was lonely but luckier than most kids because I wasn't a real orphan. I lied when I told the press that my mother was dead. It was to protect her privacy, and when news finally broke that she was in a mental hospital, I didn't lie. I told the press: I take care of my mother. I always have. I want privacy. And when the nude calendar news broke in '52, the studio thought my career would slam into a dead-end. Against their wishes, I owned up to it, saying that I needed the fifty bucks to cover my rent, and people were sympathetic. That calendar was a big boost to my career!

JANUARY 23, 1962

Dear Red,

Peter invited me to sing "Happy Birthday" to the president at Madison Square Garden on May 19, and he insists I accept. Just in case, I've already stopped eating. My new diet is grapefruit, Champagne, chicken, and vegetables. I can't go unless I lose eight pounds. My dress should be slinky, shiny, sparkly, tight, golden, and see-through! Something only Marilyn could wear. Who shall I ask to design it?

Lots of bazazz will be there—Maria Callas, Ella Fitzgerald, Peggy Lee, Bobby Darin, Jimmy Durante, Mike Nichols, Elaine May, Jack Benny, Harry Belafonte, Henry Fonda. I can't stop singing, "Happy birthday, Mr. President, Happy birthday to you!" I already called Weinstein to let Fox know I'll be off set two days. It's a big deal. I can't say no to my country.

JANUARY 24, 1962

Dear Red,

I met Henry Weinstein finally. He's a chubby, young smarty-pants, and when he made his usual telephone call to check up on me today, I put him to work: a twenty-minute crash course on American history. We wrote questions for my upcoming dinner with the general. I've never met him before!

1) What is your plan to end segregation in the South?
2) People have a moral duty to disobey unjust laws, don't they?
3) And the government's got to back them up!
4) I read about the angry mobs attacking the Freedom Riders in the South. I hope you're protecting them, Mr. General. And deal with that racist pig, Wallace!
5) Are you supporting Dr. King? I think his travels to Africa and India are fascinating.

PS: Speaking of freedom, I signed my ticket to slavery today for *Something's Got to Give*. It's being coproduced with Marilyn Monroe Productions, but the script still stinks and is still being rewritten. Shooting starts in two months. Of course, my costar, Dean Martin, is like a brother to me. He's a dream to work with. And I'm looking forward to the kids—a boy and a girl—and the pooch!

JANUARY 25, 1962

Dear Red,

Blood drips down my legs when I stand. Blood pools every time I lay down. *The River of No Return*, again! Chronic endometriosis. Doctors want to do a hysterectomy, but I still might want to have a baby one day. When I'm really down, I read Gandhi. He said lots of things about the world I agree with and makes me feel better.

No human being is perfect, but none is beyond redemption. We can only win over an opponent by love, not hate. Nonviolence is an active force—not a physical force, but of will.

Desire becomes will at a certain point, when you are able to focus. I know that because I've really only wanted three things ever since I was a little girl—to be loved, even with all my imperfections, to be respected, and above all, to be a successful actress.

JANUARY 26, 1962

Dear Red,

A fan from Nebraska says she's seen every movie of mine and she wants to be an artist. She asked me to write back using the name Delores Mills so her parents aren't suspicious. Like I'm evil! I told her what Lee says: "Art is longer than life." To be remembered, you have to do something new.

JANUARY 27, 1962

Dear Red,

People used to call me Johnny Hyde's girl. I always denied it because I wasn't in love, but he made people pay attention to me. Before Johnny, people assumed I was scheming. I'd go to parties wearing my one dress and my one pair of heels, and no one would say a word to me. Johnny was able to reach the directors, just like Joe Schneck, who got me my first contract with Twentieth Century Fox.

Pat slept the night at my house. I've been up all night reading Lorca:

I hear the song of the worm
In the heart of so many girls.
Rust, rotting, trembling earth.

The sun is coming up in the fog. The temperature is supposed to be in the mid-sixties. I need to start packing. Mrs. Murphy is coming over to help. Shit, I've lived in this apartment over ten years—I mean, in and out of marriages. It was never meant to be home.

Breakfast: three cups of black coffee
Lunch: cottage cheese and pineapple, three cups of black coffee
Dinner: bubbly and crackers like the old days

I could write a book about people who deserve a big round of applause for all the help they've given me. And what I've learned is that when someone helps, there is also the pain of moving on, as noted with Freddy Karger and with Ben Lyons, who renamed me Marilyn Monroe, using my grandmother's name. I remember Fox wrote a story that I was a babysitter when they discovered me, to make the story more sensational, as if I never considered an acting career. And here I am still working with Fox.

Then Johnny Hyde came along, someone I loved but not in the romantic sense. Someone who gave me his all. He called me Miss Caswell because of the role I played in *All About Eve*. He was vice president of William Morris Agency and worked behind the scenes to mold my long-term career. He got me into every audition that was right for me. I paid him his agent's fee, and he paid for my clothes and acting lessons and spending money and plastic surgery for my chin. It was a little too round, so I had it thinned a bit. My front teeth needed a cap to cover the slight gap. My nose was a tiny bit too turned up—too much of a bump at the tip—so I had it adjusted. Johnny was thirty years older than me, and he had a bad heart. He knew he would die soon and wanted me to marry him so I would be financially secure. I told him I wasn't digging for gold. He was my best friend, and it broke my heart to say it, but I wasn't in love with him. When he died, I felt so alone. His family hated me and wouldn't let me take my things from his house or say goodbye to him. So I snuck in at night to give him a kiss. Then after the funeral, I was so sad and lonely to lose such a friend that I swallowed all the pills I had. It's the only time I ever deliberately tried to kill myself. My roommate found me and got me to the hospital to have my stomach pumped.

January 28, 1962

Dear Red,

This morning I ran three miles through the alleyways of Hollywood. I love to run and sweat and feel free—head, shoulders, spine, hips, everything is about hips. If I wake up feeling good, I want to run. By night I don't care anymore.

I'm throwing out gobs of stuff, finding stuff to keep, packing other stuff—dresses, pedal pushers, swimsuits, and shoes—clothing that was given to me for the most part. My stepsister Bernice and her daughter in Florida might like it. You wouldn't think a girl could squish so much into closets!

January 29, 1962

Dear Red,

I'm so tired! Eunice Murray helped me pack up my books. It's not the kind of exercise I like, but we talked about furnishings for the house. I'm excited and nostalgic at the same time. What would that look like? Half a smile? The head tilted to the non-smiling side. Arms out. Legs together. Ankles crossed.

January 30, 1962

Dear Red,

Gee, tonight is our last dinner in my apartment. Rafe likes to grill on my itty-bitty balcony rather than eat out. He's sexy and affectionate, and we like to dance to records in my living room. We're both attracted to men, so instead of having sex, we talk about it.

Briggs Deli order:

One sirloin steak
One chicken cutlet
Potatoes
Caviar
Crackers
Dom Perignon
Butter
Iceberg lettuce
Tomato
Cucumber
No dessert, we're dieting

January 31, 1962

Dear Red,

I've been marking up the script for Nunnally's rewrite of *Something's Got to Give*. I'm Ellen. I've been stranded on a desert island for five years, and now I have to convince my husband to take me back. Ellen needs to be a fully realized character. The comedy is not in the words but the timing.

The kids didn't remember me—only the dog. His name is Tippy. I named him after my childhood puppy. Isn't that sweet, Maf? You understand. Dogs like me. Working with kids and dogs are a natural for me. And I'm working with some of my favorites, like Dean Martin and Wally Cox. Cyd Charisse might be challenging, however.

Lemon is a daisy color, crayon yellow. Lemon is oval, like an egg with a nipple! Lemon has tanned leather like an old man slathered in aftershave. The juice bites like ocean salt. Like bitter cactus, or too sweet fig, it makes my jaw ache. I suck the sticky tartness, roll it under my arms, and squeeze it over my neck and breasts and suck the juice in the shade out by my pool.

I pull the fiber out and chew it like a goat or a camel. I chew the whole bitter outer peel into tiny bits—my lips buzz and go numb. Pretty soon, I've eaten the whole thing!

February 1, 1962

Dear Red,

Goodbye forever, Doheny Drive! Hello, Helena Drive! Three bedrooms, white walls, fireplace, an oval pool. Eunice Murray starts tomorrow as my housekeeper. She agreed to drive me around in her green Dodge to do errands at City National Bank, Briggs Deli, and the pharmacy. I don't have a car these days and rely on a limo service.

Why did it take me so long to buy a house by myself? It's no lonelier than renting an apartment. I sketched a whole wall of bookshelves for Mrs. Murray's son, Ray, to build. And he will line my closet with shelves and build kitchen cabinets and a breakfast table and benches like Dr. G has in his kitchen. I told Ray I want a brick floor, like in Mexico, too. And he can redo the fireplace with Mexican tiles. The new appliances will be installed while I'm in Mexico. Tonight I'm going to the Lawfords' to meet the general and his wife!

February 2, 1962

Dear Red,

Dad asked, "Bubbeleh, did the general love you?"

"Uh huh," I said. "And what I like best about him, besides his civil rights program, is his sense of humor. And he knows everyone at Fox. He's doing a film with Budd Schulberg—*The Enemy Within*. Weinstein offered to help me study for the next date with the General, but I told him I don't need any more help."

"Atta girl, Marilyn," Dad said, and blew me a kitzl.

Then I asked Dad if he would he like to be my date for Dreamboat's birthday bash at Madison Square Garden. I told him I would like to introduce him to the president. He said he would be honored to be my date, he really would. I said, "Okay. It's May 19. Get a plane ticket to New York."

Last night Pat Lawford served the cutest round roasted potatoes, carved with a fruit scoop! I played with her kids—cards, Frisbee, jump rope—while she cooked. She gives the nanny one week off a month so she can do the whole mothering thing herself. After the first day, she moves the clock ahead and puts the kids to bed an hour early every night, she's so tired! And she confessed that last year, after the baby was born, she rented an apartment across the street for the nanny and baby so the rest of the family could sleep! After dinner the two of us walked the dark Santa Monica beach. She said my fans are missing the best part of me, and the press has me all wrong: Marilyn is smart, fun, funny, and warm. I said, "No, the press has me exactly where they want me: lo-bottom-ized!"

February 3, 1962

Dear Red,

I told Rafe he looked like Johnny Weissmuller in *Tarzan*, swinging from room to room with boxes on his shoulders. He doesn't like Dr. G and my new housekeeper, Mrs. Murray—she's Dr. G's friend. So is Rudin, my new attorney, come to think of it. Mrs. Murray is helpful but not warm. I get the feeling she likes to pretend she's my mother, and a diary lying around is an invitation to snoop. I made that mistake with Arthur! Where, oh where, can a hiding place be? Not under the mattress or in a drawer. I need to buy something that locks, like a combination safe I can keep in the guest room. In the meantime, I have to carry Red with me and train Mrs. Murray to stay out of my room when I'm not home! I talk on the phone into the wee hours, so when I say good-night, I take the phone in my room—it's got an extra-long cord—and when I sleep I put a pillow over it so I won't hear it ring.

I hid a house key in the flowerpot hanging by the front door and told Peter and Dr. E, my physician. And my bedroom door is never locked.

FEBRUARY 4, 1962

Dear Red,

It takes work to be Marilyn! I'm lucky I've got a lot of help. Whitey, my makeup magician, grinds his own oils and powders from Max Factor. He can take five or more hours for special occasions, and he doesn't mind starting while I'm asleep. He married my wardrobe mistress, Marjorie. A beautiful couple. I adore them both! I gave Whitey a cigarette case that says "While I'm still warm," a reminder to fix me up in case something happens.

Eight celestial bodies are lining up—sun, moon, Mercury, Venus, Mars, Jupiter, Saturn, and Earth. It's lucky! But so far, nothing special is happening to me. Agnes is doing my hair—I adore her children. That reminds me, I want to send them a swing set she told me about. Pearl sometimes does my hair. She worked with Jean Harlow and Mae West. The general gave me Mickey Song's phone number the other day—hair dresser for Raquel Welch. I'll put him on my list. God knows, there are days when I'm desperate for help.

Pat paid *Confidential* $500 to keep my new house out of the paper—let the realtor sizzle. When she started rattling off the names of my neighbors, like Julie Andrews, Phyllis Diller, Bette Davis, Angela Lansbury, Joan

Crawford, and Peter Lorre, I made it clear that I want my privacy. I told her I don't want to know who my neighbors are. That's why I like the seven-foot wall around the house. And I like the address—12305 Fifth Helena Drive—just missing the four.

I've lived so many places in my life, but this move feels different than my apartment in New York. There I usually like to say hello to my neighbors, but here all I want is my privacy, a garden, a quiet garden where I can be alone.

FEBRUARY 5, 1962

Dear Red,

I came out of my bedroom around 10:30, after I said goodnight to Mrs. Murray, and there she was gossiping with Henry Weinstein! I didn't have any clothes on, and they groaned and covered their eyes like I was a hideous monster. I told Mrs. Murray I don't see the point of clothes at home, and she'll have to get used to it. But what were they talking about in my house? He stopped by to say hello, he said. Fuck! Yet another of Dr. G's friends who "manage" me. I turned up Louie Armstrong full blast.

Three hours later, I'm wide awake. I'm feeling surrounded. All Ring around the Rosie. Twentieth Century Fox, housekeeper, doctor, lawyer, and handyman. I hope this doesn't turn out to be like the bubonic plague.

FEBRUARY 6, 1962

Dear Red,

Stand as if god is holding you up by your hair. This way your neck is completely straight, at ease, and your head sits on your spine. Shoulders float over your torso. Spine sits on pelvis. Pelvis moves between legs and spine. Arms swing, legs swing, hips swivel, swing, snap. You can practice this any time of day, every time you walk.

Joe Junior is engaged. I don't like the girl much. I met her last year in Florida. He sensed I wasn't thrilled at lunch today, and he asked me to tell him the truth. I said, "I hope she loves you enough," and he tried to reassure me. Of course, I don't have a good marriage record, so it's kind of difficult for him to take advice from me. But I told him love is the only reason two people should marry, even though most people marry for all kinds of reasons. Joey has to be careful or he's going to get himself hurt. Even though I'm just an ex-stepmother, he listens.

February 7, 1962

Dear Red,

Great
fruit is grape-
fruit—a tart way
to start the day,
especially
if a girl aims to marry
the president.

When I'm tired, nervous, and worried, I stutter, and if I spend forty-five minutes on the coffee cup exercise, I can make the stutter go away. I learned this before I studied at the studio. I remember the very first coffee cup exercise in 1955. Imagination is one of my best talents. Someone had to shake me when it was time to do the scene work. Today I used my favorite Mexican cup with the heavy blue glaze because it feels smooth on my tongue and it's not too fat between my lips. My left hand curves with the cup, and my right hand grips the handle. Face, hands, nose, breasts—all of me—crouching over the dark, hot, deep South American coffee smell. It's a pick-me-up! The buzz races through me like jagged lightning, all the way to the tips of my fingers and toes. I know I probably drink too much of it, but so nu?

I was shocked at the photographs of women around the world in the *National Geographic*—their natural beauty and liberation regarding clothes. Some African tribes don't cover their breasts and it is perfectly acceptable. Gee, was I born in the wrong place! Others wear the most colorful cloth draped around their heads and torsos like Romans. I can't image how they get it to stay on while they carry babies and water and gather firewood. Some cover up all but their eyes. If I could dress however I wanted, I'd cover my eyes in sunglasses and leave the rest naked.

February 8, 1962

Dear Red,

Arthur Jacobs called today. Pat's boss. Pat books my monthly press conferences, magazine interviews, and charity events while Arthur feeds the press. He's skilled in love too. His fairy-tale beautiful girlfriend Natalie was younger than me with my first marriage when he proposed— she was fourteen! But he's politely waited for her to grow up! They recently announced their engagement, now that she's eighteen. Isn't that romantic! I've got years and years to wait for Dreamboat.

February 9, 1962

Dear Red,

I'm spread naked on the chaise lounge by the pool in the shade, pen in hand. I feel calm. Simply feeling *me*. Writing words down on a page strangely connects me to that great big community of writers that came before, like Sappho, Rilke, Anne Frank, and the Wife of Bath, and I feel less lonely. I'm sure I'll make some discoveries about myself, but in the meantime, it's good to get the old brain exercised. I'm faithful, Red. I love you.

Maf is practicing his fly-swallowing techniques. Jump! Clap! Snap! I think it's the buzz that drives him dizzy, not hunger. I'm afraid if he gets good enough, he'll run away and join the circus!

PoETic fly, GO
You BUZZ my Dog!
aWAY big FLY
Or I'll PLAY you DIZzy
GillESpie!

FEBRUARY 10, 1962

Dear Red,

Brando and I went incognito to the 4:00 show of *Mutiny on the Bounty*. We snuck into the theater when the lights went down and snuggled in the back like newlyweds. He pointed out the new wide-screen process—it looks so real. *Misfits* was wide screen too. He told me he's marrying the young Tahitian love interest in the film on August 10! "Gee," I told him, "she's beautiful!" After the show we fooled around back at his mansion. I told him about my diary, and he said one day he plans to write about his aunt who raised him. We don't see each other much, but we share blood.

FEBRUARY 11, 1962

Dear Red,

I asked Dreamboat if he was working on equality for women. He said he made a deal with Eleanor Roosevelt before the election that he'd start a commission on the status of women, and he has.

Government change is slow, but look how a single person like Margaret Sanger started a revolution by tackling unwanted pregnancy, and the consequences on poverty, hunger, and the opportunity for women to get educated and have a career. He called me a leader for social change, too—I'm part of the sexual revolution.

"You mean it's our patriotic duty to make love?" I asked.

"Absolutely," he said.

Practice
Makes Perfect
And Freedom
Takes Practice even though
Freedom, like Love,
Is not Perfect
It's worth it!

February 12, 1962

Dear Red,

Truman is writing a new book. When I asked if it had a happy ending, he said an upcoming trial will determine the ending. He's depressed. He isn't into the new year. He's cold and alone in New York. I warmed him up with the memory of us dancing nude at Cecil Beaton's party last year. He's still sore I didn't get to play Holly Golightly. He wrote the part for me, but I was locked in a contract with Fox, and Paramount couldn't pay enough to release me.

Audrey is adorable, but even my agent agreed that the story is all foreplay between a young woman and her teacher, like it is too sexual for American audiences, and too sexual a role for me! What nonsense. Will it take another thousand years of evolution before it's acceptable for women to be sexual human beings?

It is only day twelve, and I got into a nasty argument with Mrs. Murray. She's like an automaton! She treats me like I'm a glass vase. Her body language shouts her real feelings. When I call her on it, she freezes like a statue. She said Dr. G told her to spend the night. I told her to go home.

"Who is your boss?" I asked.

"Dr. Greenson."

"Who pays you?"

"You do."

"So who is your boss?" I opened the front door. "I'll see you tomorrow at eight a.m.," I said.

After Mrs. Murphy left, I put on Ella Fitzgerald and realized it was Lincoln's birthday! I kissed his photograph on my mantel and lit a candle for my two favorite presidents. Maf got excited by my little dance and wanted to wrestle, so I put on potholder mitts—his little teeth are sharp!

February 13, 1962

Dear Red,

I love my private walled garden with bougainvillea, palm trees, and flowering bushes. I'm so happy to walk outside with the birds and trees. They were my imaginary playmates growing up. I lived in my own natural world, and most of the time, I didn't know what the kids were talking about. Oh, I was good at softball, but walking to school, flowers were little mysteries I could watch every day and never solve. It's time to hire a gardener!

On blue-sky days in Connecticut, I used to lie on top of the picnic table and watch the drama of clouds, always changing shapes. Imagine, wisps of water vapor decorate the sky! In Los Angeles, the morning fog clears to blue sky by noon, flowers bloom most of the year, but there are no watery drawings to study.

Joe Jr. called upset. His bosses make him go along with their lies. The employees are locked into their jobs and don't have a choice. Confrontation might get him fired, but collaborating makes him feel trapped. I suggested that he tell his boss to go to hell. Just say your stepmom said so. I told him to use my name.

Breakfast: black coffee
Lunch: black coffee
Dinner: bubbly, caviar, oysters, lobster

FEBRUARY 14, 1962

Dear Red,

Jackie gave a televised tour of the White House using my breathy voice! Pat Lawford was outraged Jackie was so phony, but Peter and I thought it was hilarious. I have the White House phone number, and Jackie and I speak every now and then, so she knows what I sound like. Tomorrow I'm marching out to buy myself a pillbox hat! Actually, I think Jackie's a good sport. Joe sent me two dozen red roses. "To Marilyn, my true love. xxx Joe." He still loves me.

When Dreamboat called tonight and he said my name, I sang, *"Hap*-py *birth-*day *to* you," and he said, "No, Marilyn! No, Marilyn!" pretending I was giving him an orgasm. Or maybe he wasn't pretending. We've always conducted electricity.

FEBRUARY 15, 1962

Dear Red,

I asked my driver to stop at the side of 101 yesterday to watch the sun set from the limo. Sometimes I just like to step on the gas. Maybe I need a little car like the one Arthur gave me— that sporty black Thunderbird. I loved to drive up the Taconic to the Connecticut farm, the clean air blowing the cobwebs out of my head. Virginia Dennison came over this morning to teach me Hatha yoga—maybe *that* will clear the cobwebs. I was exhausted after one hour, and my legs are sore. I've always known yoga is good for my legs.

I asked Mrs. Murray to drive me to Gladys Lindberg's Health Food store in Long Beach and told her to please wait in the car. I wanted to consult with Gladys. I'm nervous because whenever I work on a film, I get so run down with the stress I end up with a sinus infection, or worse. I'd met her briefly once before at the Dennisons' party. She's in her forties, a beatnik with beads, long gray hair, and a pretty, direct style. I told her my mother's name is Gladys, and in fact, she was like a doctor asking me for a whole rundown of drugs, food, habits. I told her a brief history of hospitalizations, my insomnia, and endometriosis. She's familiar with the film industry and just how difficult *The Misfits* was. I told her I ended up in the hospital and I don't want that to happen again. She walked around her store gathering brewer's yeast and a dozen herbs and pills, fish oil, things I can't get at Schwab's or Brent-Air pharmacy. And she pulled Adelle Davis's book *Let's Eat Right to Keep Fit* off her bookshelf. It's just a little paperback, but she said, it's an important book. She took my hands in hers and looked into each of my eyes. She said I looked like I was running on empty. Cut down on the coffee. Cut out the enemas— those are not natural, not necessary, and not good for your body. Refuse the "vitamin" shots the studios force on actors. She said they were not vitamins but a whole mix of drug, and dangerous, especially mixed with alcohol. With all the other pills floating around, she said she is amazed we are able to work. I usually just blow off that kind of advice—I mean, I've been doing that shit for years—but I have respect for Gladys Lindberg.

Sometimes writing things down makes aspects of my life sound dire. I guess I need to take responsibility, or at least think twice about my choices. Fox doesn't know what's good for me.

FEBRUARY 16, 1962

Dear Red,

Arthur married Inge Morath today. I should be happy, right? But I think of them enjoying the Connecticut farm and it depresses me. They flirted on the set as we shot *Misfits*. Meanwhile he kept rewriting the script using my angry words. I felt so used and exposed. We knew our marriage was over, but why did the pain have to be so public? Only I got blamed for problems on the set—the dumb blond is an easy scapegoat.

Clark Gable was a sweetie, letting me cry on his shoulder at Bucket of Blood Saloon. I was so sad when he died a few months later, his wife pregnant. Of course people blamed me for his death! He was the only cast member who never complained when I blew a line. When I was little, Mother gave me a photograph of Clark Gable—she told me he was the spitting image of my father.

Come to think of it, I also got blamed on the set of *Let's Make Love*. Yves Montand told gossip columnist Hedda Hopper that I wooed him, when Montand was the one who chased after Cukor *and* me, playing us off each other. We got along better before Montand came along. I never bothered to correct his lie. Montand got the American press he wanted, making me the slut. Like Arthur, who let the press babble on, never mentioning that *he* was the one to have an affair. I was loyal to Arthur. And I've never been a tattletale.

Doris Day sings "Que Sera Sera" bullshit on the radio all day long.

I'm drawing sketches, looking through magazines, trying to decide what kind of hairdo I want for the president's birthday. My hair has been a different blonde in each of my films: moonlight, golden ash, silver ash, white ash, amber, smoky blonde, honey white, topaz white, unbleached, platinum white, and now pillowcase.

February 17, 1962

Dear Red,

I woke up to the same bad dream—smoke seeps from beneath the closet door, and my muscles spasm up and down my left side. I called Inez right away, afraid something happened to Mother. She visited this week and assured me that Mother is fine. I've got a trust fund for Mother's care at the Rockhaven Sanitarium. It should be enough if she lives to be a hundred. But after talking to Inez, my voice was still shaky, and I called Dr. E. He came over and gave me a shot to calm me down. Even now, hours later, I am still trembling. I feel like the wild horses in *Misfits* about to be turned into dog food.

February 18, 1962

Dear Red,

It's 3:21. I soaked in the bath, took pills, and still can't sleep. This afternoon, we were on Santa Monica Boulevard, a few blocks from my house. I was putting on lipstick and looking in the mirror and saw Giancana in the passenger seat of the car behind us. A woman was driving. I pointed him out to Mrs. Murray. If you ever see him again, tell me. She asked who he was. I just said, "A friend of a friend."

Gandhi called his autobiography experiments with truth. Reading about his life as it evolved is like reincarnation. I think he started out as an accountant! Truth is a kind of balance you have to practice, like walking. A continual adjustment is necessary to come up with the truth.

FEBRUARY 19, 1962

Dear Red,

The Rat Pack doesn't consider my belt full of notches equal to theirs, but Frankie can't get rid of his feelings for me. And he can't make me disappear like all the other girls. That's why they call me an institution, like his mother, Dolly. She was godmother of Hoboken, saving neighbors down on their luck, including a Jewish girl in need of surgery. Dolly told me that she always wanted a little girl, but Frankie was her only kid.

I woke up with blood all over the bed like something violent happened. I hate that women have to put up with feeling bloated, the cramps, the painkillers, and the mess. Being born a man might have been better for a lot of reasons, but then I should accept all the parts of womanhood, right?

Dad and I don't agree on everything. I mean, there is nearly a forty-year age difference. He thinks Adelle Davis is bullshit. She says that every day you do one of two things: you build a healthy body, or you produce disease. I'd rather call it dis-ease. I think she speaks the truth, but I don't argue with him. Fathers are of a different generation, and truth seems to change with time. Old movies have to be remade. Just look at the Adam and Eve story—that old script needs a major rewrite!

FEBRUARY 20, 1962

Dear Red,

I've always adopted families. Lately it's Dr. G's. I like his kids and his Spanish-style house. But I have a house of my own now. I don't need his. I think all he needs is one big fat patient—Marilyn Monroe—for his livelihood. He takes so much of my time—ninety minutes every morning. And since I moved, he stops by my house for no reason. Maybe my upcoming trip to Mexico will break his bad habit.

To-Do List

1) Ask Dr. G how to get a new fantasy (he needs it)

FEBRUARY 21, 1962

Dear Red,

Astronaut John Glenn circled the earth three times today, and the whole world stopped. Isn't that something? Seven thousand people watched on a screen in Grand Central Station. The capsule dropped into the ocean and was picked up by a destroyer. That is fucking dramatic! Dreamboat greeted Glenn at Cape Canaveral and invited him to the White House to hear what it was like to float in space. I look forward to the picture of earth whispered in my ear one day soon.

FEBRUARY 22, 1962

Dear Red,

Sh'ma Yisrael. I'm off to Mexico City with Pat and Mrs. Murray to shop for furniture. We booked rooms at the Continental Hilton Hotel. Freddy Field and his wife Nieves will be our guides, friends of Bacall. I met them years ago shooting *How to Marry a Millionaire*. Freddy tells stories about the Vanderbilts, who disowned him, and his escapades as a communist archeologist. Everyone thinks he's a fool for giving up all that family money. I disagree—living my dream is more fun than living someone else's.

FEBRUARY 23, 1962

Dear Red,

Freddy had a luscious reception for us! Artists, politicians, musicians, and colorful dancers in an outdoor garden with fruity drinks, Cuban cigars, roasted goat on a spit (which I couldn't look at), piñatas, and confetti. Everyone's talking about peyote, a desert cactus, drug of the Aztecs, but my head is in the toilet. The doctor says it's the altitude and the heat that's making me dizzy. So, I'm dozing, thumbing magazines all day long, and drinking lots of quinine water imported from France, and lime juice.

FEBRUARY 24, 1962

Dear Red,

All I can do is lounge in the shade at the pool. I'm thinking about Mother, born in Diaz, Mexico. I wish I knew her as a young woman, before her husband stole her first two children and destroyed her spirit. She chased them down, but when she saw how happy they were, she let them be. She found a job as a nanny for a little girl named Norma Jeane! That's where she got my name. When I was born, she worked as a film-cutter to pay my childcare, but she never really recovered. Dreamboat said marriage was a disappointment for his mother too.

The clouds look like wings galloping across the blue. That's where God and the angels must have come from. Humans, flat on their backs, looking up at the sky, imagining that someone was up there looking out for them.

FEBRUARY 25, 1962

Dear Red,

The dark horse Jose came over for drinks and was more charming than I remembered! Kahlo's La Casa Azul in Coyoacan is like a chapel with her ashes in an urn on the mantel. Diego's studio was upstairs, but the door was locked. I was drawn to her self-portraits but wanted to cry looking at *The Wounded Deer*. Diego in her arms like a big baby made me laugh— some men are big babies! Jose said she loved children but was impaled by metal through her uterus in a bus crash and mostly painted from bed. I made the sign of the cross for Santa Frida.

FEBRUARY 26, 1962

Dear Red,

I took my diary along with me today so I could write these names down. It amused Jose! Paso de la Reforma is tree-lined like the Champs-Elysees with embassies, the Monument to the Revolution with four arches, the Angel of Independence, and the Museum of Modern Art. We saw the social realist frescos of Jose Orozco and Diego Rivera and Bravo's photograph of a bloody corpse in the sun. My stomach still doesn't feel so good.

FEBRUARY 27, 1962

Dear Red,

Bolanos lives in beautiful Las Lomas with streets named after mountains, and the houses are walled mansions. Grasshopper Hill Park is a palace built by the Aztec poet-king Montezuma. His mother had an immaculate conception—she swallowed a hollow arrow containing jewels that flew over the palace wall. Gee, that's imaginative! At the zoo we saw a chimpanzee flex his arm muscle like a he-man, lustful, tender monkeys not just copulating but performing oral sex on each other. We also saw a mother orangutan holding her baby. We stayed real still so we could see how the baby's face is always moving. I showed him how I practice that in the mirror every day. I can even wiggle my tail!

As I get older, giving means more than just receiving. They're intertwined. Giving isn't the same as receiving, and giving isn't enough. But Jose is a gentleman. He insists on women first when it comes to love making.

FEBRUARY 28, 1962

Dear Red,

I never think of you as communist. I won't give up the nickname. Besides, it *is* your color. Red should be free of political meaning. Red is apple. Sunsets. Lips. Blood. Mother's hair—well, she dyed it like Jean Harlow. We shopped after lunch and ended up at Tina Modotti's grave. A romantic and a revolutionary, Jose said. She was blamed in the attempted murder of the Mexican president and was said to have died of heart failure after assisting in the Spanish Civil War. At least Neruda gave her the respect she deserved. He wrote her a beautiful epitaph:

> *bees, shadows, fire, snow, silence, foam*
> *combined with steel and wire and pollen*
> *make up your firm and delicate being.*

MARCH 1, 1962

Dear Red,

A plane crashed on takeoff near Idlewild Airport today, killing all eight-seven passengers! It's scary to think how many times I've taken off from there without saying the Sh'ma or even a Hail Mary. I always went to church with Joe when we were married, and when I was little, it was Baptists, Christian Scientists, or Jehovah's Witnesses. Nobody understands how I connect with the Jews who are the intellectual storytellers—the underdog. Isn't it strange that people think that being smart is a problem!

Good news, I lost five pounds in Mexico. Jeanne Carmen met me in the steam room so I could shed those last three pounds. She says the worst thing is a flat ass like hers. Mine's a little extra big, so I wouldn't know. I said, "Sexy comes from the inside." We had a fight because she didn't believe me, so I showed her two ways of walking—Marilyn, and not Marilyn.

MARCH 2, 1962

Dear Red,

The Walt Disney Company called to say they created Tinkerbell in my image! She's mother of the lost boys and spreads fairy dust in Never Never Land! Disney wants to know what kind of royalties I want. I told Frosch to send them a letter saying I'm flattered. I don't want to make money off Tinkerbell. Joe says I'm foolish to turn away money. I asked him to take me on a long drive into the desert, but he wants to sit home and watch sports on TV.

I met with the Swedish tutor today—an actress who has a real ear for accents. "Pretend there are three marbles in your mouth," she said, "and the marbles are moving around your tongue. Be very careful that you do not swallow them when you talk." That's what speaking English with a Swedish accent is like. A light singsong, with a little French curl.

MARCH 3, 1962

Dear Red,

My Hulda Dombek customized bras arrived! They're like pyramids in black, red, coral, and sky blue! For sleeping, of course. I wouldn't dream of wearing something like that under a dress— people want to look at me, not a bra. Louella Parsons interviewed me at two o'clock for *Look*. She said Barbara Stanwyck calls me the "carefree kid who owns the world." I said there are lots of bright stars out there, and we're all kind of lonely and hungry, so we may seem like kids. It's the fans that keep us hot. As for owning the world, it's only on loan.

Breakfast: black coffee and herbs from my garden
Lunch: gefilte fish on cracker with horseradish and apple slices
Dinner: oysters and bubbly

MARCH 4, 1962

Dear Red,

Unpacking books is like saying hello to old friends. I counted more than four hundred—many from my literature classes at UCLA eleven years ago. I found Arthur's *Death of a Salesman*: "1954, To Marilyn, with admiration, Arthur Miller." That was the night I escorted him to Kazan's party. And *The Complete Shakespeare*, from Olivier—"For the Marilyn Monroe Shakespeare Company." We didn't get along in the end, but I sure respect his Hamlet. My Shakespeare Company is still a good plan—something to start when I turn forty. Or sooner.

I found my leather-bound copy of *Leaves of Grass*. I used it as a prop in many auditions. There's a bunch of classics—*Catcher in the Rye, Lady Chatterley's Lover, Uncle Tom's Cabin, A Tale of Two Cities, The Jungle.* John Hersey's *Hiroshima*—I couldn't read that again. Freud, Rilke, Shelley, Keats. The biographies of Duse and Eleanor Roosevelt. *King James Bible*—that's a good script. *Catch-22, The Diary of Anne Frank, The Joy of Cooking*—that goes in the kitchen. Plato's *The Last Days of Socrates, Howl, The Invisible Man. The Thinking Body!* I spent a good hour rereading my notes in the margin. Mable Dodge: "Old age is not measured chronologically. One becomes old when habits are set permanently, when the formation of new habits is no longer welcome."

On June 1 I turn thirty-six. It's a scary curve, hopefully not a corner. But why am I afraid of getting old? If you don't live a long life, how can you ever really know how wonderful you can be? Not wanting to grow old is just another one of those myths that needs to be unlearned.

Aunt Ana's Christian Science prayer book—I can't read it, and I can't toss it. She wrote: "Dear Norma, read this book. I don't leave you much except my love, but not even death can diminish that; nor will death ever take me far away from you." I wrote her a love poem in reply after she died. I thought I stuck it in her prayer book, but I don't see it here. I wish I had it.

My dog-eared *Wife of Bath*! "What women want most is independent power over men, love, and God." I agree, only today I crossed out "men, love, and God" and wrote "themselves." I underlined it three times. What women want most is independent power over themselves!

I found boxes of fan mail from the US servicemen I sang for in Korea. I called Dad and read him some over the phone. Gee, the letters still give me goose bumps—lonely boys really too young to be fighting, so wrong to be dying.

MARCH 5, 1962

Dear Red,

Going to the Golden Globe Awards tonight. Elizabeth Arden Salon gave me a three-hour head-to-toe massage and beauty treatment in my living room! Hair is done. Whitey will be here any minute to do my makeup. I'm wearing a beautiful green beaded dress with no back. Apparently, Jose and Freddy Vanderbilt had a falling out over politics. Oh, well. Jose is a sweetheart to escort me—I've paid my dues as stand-ins. I'm grateful to be nominated for the award, but I wonder if anyone will be there for me.

MARCH 6, 1962

Dear Red,

All the stars were twinkling! Not the usual merry-go-round. I was a little tipsy because I didn't eat for two days and gulped two glasses of Champagne once we arrived. We didn't stay long. I must have sweated those last three pounds because this morning, after coffee, I weighed 117—a perfect weight for me. Maybe it's all those enemas. Just in time for the screen tests today for *Something's Got to Give*. The cameraman said the pillow white hair color looked fine when I asked him. Bright like my skin, he said.

MARCH 7, 1962

Dear Red,

My second meeting with Dreamboat was in 1953. He said, "You've become a big star since we met. I think of you every day."

"That makes two of us," I said, "but you're engaged!"

He said, "I'm running for president of the United States in 1960, and I can't get elected as a bachelor."

"So," I asked, "is this good-bye?"

"No, Marilyn, we've got a whole lifetime."

"Gee," I said, "somehow I don't believe you."

He said, "My father taught me that sometimes a man's wife is not the love of his life."

That's when I fell in love with him. Walking barefoot on the beach, he recited Keats to explain how he felt about serving the public: *Those who feel the agony of the world, and more, like slaves to poor humanity, labor for mortal good* … "That's heroic," I said. "What about Jackie? Do you love her? Because I think love is the only reason to marry."

"Jacqueline will make a wonderful wife. She is beautiful, she is Catholic, and she is an intelligent woman. America has never elected a Catholic, but the time has come."

He told me about his father and Gloria Swanson. Gloria and her husband visited often, and Joe took Gloria sailing every day. Jack as a twelve-year-old couldn't understand why he couldn't go sailing, too, so he stowed away. When he caught them in each other's arms, he jumped overboard, and his father went after him. That's when he explained that a man needs to get laid every day.

I said, "That's unusual advice from a father—or it would be for a girl, anyway."

MARCH 8, 1962

Dear Red,

I took Tashi by my favorite girlhood lemon tree on Odessa Street, and it was blooming! He is teaching me to garden. We bought lots of perennials and herbs and started planting before it got too hot. My gloves were full of dirt when Maf started barking, and I ignored him until I realized he had fallen in the pool! Tashi jumped in and rescued Maf, and Mrs. Murphy found him some dry clothes that made Tashi look like the murderer in *Rear Window*. I laughed so hard. I towel dried Maf and fed him my lunch of salmon, scolding him all the while about going fishing!

Tonight, after editing Nunnally's rewrites, I have decided to swim naked in the pool scene instead of looking like a drowned pooch in a fake nude suit. Shh. It's a secret.

Joe and I saw real hula dancers on our honeymoon during our Hawaiian stopover to Japan. The dancers moved their hips without hoops, naked except for thick grass skirts and beautiful orchid leis. They danced with their eyes closed, breasts gyrating as their arms floated up in ecstasy.

MARCH 9, 1962

Dear Red,

I like my hair in a flip, but in an hour Agnes is coming over to cut it short for the film. Remembering Hawaii, I bought a dozen colored hula hoops—I haven't gotten back into a routine since gallbladder surgery last year. So I blasted the radio and tried every color out by the pool. I spun the turquoise hoop for twenty-six minutes without dropping!

I'm impatient for my furniture on the slow boat from Mexico. I don't understand why shipping a table takes more than six weeks! I want to host a quiet dinner party, just the two of us! I love the happy birds in my garden, but Rachel Carson wrote that songbirds are disappearing from North America because everyone uses the chemical DDT. Sometimes the birds sing on the telephone wire or on a branch while I'm talking on the phone. I sing back *"Hap-py Birth-day"* to them. Tashi said he doesn't believe in using poison in his gardens. I'll give him my copy of *Silent Spring*. Like *Hiroshima*, it's too depressing for me.

MARCH 10, 1962

Dear Red,

I'm just home from an all-night party at the Dennisons'—not a typical Hollywood party. The house is on a cliff above a sparkling reservoir. I watched the sun rise with a lot of long-haired beatnik intellectuals— doctors talking philosophy, artists talking about the Adelle Davis, scientists talking about psychedelic drugs, farmers' rights, and human rights. I met Huxley. Disney didn't like his *Alice in Wonderland* screenplay, says he's done with Hollywood. It's noon, and I'm stuttering I'm so tired. I'm in bed but my head won't stop. I haven't slept yet.

The other day I borrowed Mrs. Murray's car and stopped to pick up my friend Shelley. She was trying to give her daughter an enema on doctor's orders, and the girl was crying hysterically. So I whispered a story to her about when my pooch Maf ate a whole chicken and his belly hurt, the doctor made him feel all better. I suggested that she roll on her side and put her paws out—and by that time, it was over!

MARCH 11, 1962

Dear Red,

The late night yesterday really turned me upside down. It's four in the morning and my mind is *on*, my body *off*. No one's ass for me to put my hand on. No one to call. No god to pray to. No soft child's breath next to mine. Aunt Ana used to hold me for dear life sometimes. My only warm spot is Frankie's gift, my sweet little pooch Maf. And a lullaby to sing, but that only excites me: *Happy birthday to you! Happy birthday to you! Happy birthday, Mr. President* ... I have to turn it into a lullaby and rock my brain to sleep. *Happy birthday to you. Happy birthday to you. Happy birthday, Mr. President. Happy birthday to you. Happy birthday to you. Happy birthday to you. Happy birthday, Mr. President. Happy birthday to you. Happy birthday to you. Happy birthday to you. Happy birthday, Mr. President. Happy birthday to you. Happy birthday to you. Happy birthday to you. Happy birthday, Mr. President. Happy birthday to you. Happy birthday to you. Happy birthday to you. Happy birthday, Mr. President. Happy birthday to you. Happy birthday to you. Happy birthday to you. Happy birthday, Mr. President. Happy birthday to you. Happy birthday to you. Happy birthday to you. Happy birthday, Mr. President. Happy birthday to you. Happy birthday to you. Happy birthday, Mr. President. Happy birthday to you.*

MARCH 12, 1962

Dear Red,

Reading scripts by the pool, Pat said she wanted to set up a photo session with *Vogue*. I stuck out my tongue. She said women like to look at women!

"I don't want to model clothes," I said.

"You are looking better than ever," she admitted. "It must be all that yoga and yogurt and brewer's yeast!"

"I quit cigarettes," I said.

"Shut up," she said. "I like to smoke."

She said she'd call Bert Stern or Eve Arnold— they've both been bugging her to schedule a photo shoot. Not *Playboy*, the slobs. "Schedule them all," I said. "And tell Bert I want to do a shoot in a church. That was my fantasy as a kid, like Jesus. The female body should be praised."

Speaking of church, Joe asked me to accompany him to Easter services with his family in San Francisco. I don't know. I said I'd have to think about it. For me, going to church was a wifely duty.

A TV commercial advertises a girdle with special fingertips to press the belly flat, as if curves are bad. And Cross My Heart bras, as if bras tell the truth! I hope women know better than to believe that shit! Nobody wants to see undergarments when they look at a woman's body. A natural look is much more alluring. When I want to stand tall and beautiful, I say think like a tree!

March 13, 1962

Dear Red,

I called Kenny, my favorite astrologer, about doing a special reading for my thirty-sixth birthday. I'm getting *old*! In the magnifying mirror, I see seven little lines around each eye. I mean, I admit, they're from smiling, so how bad is that? I noticed while talking to Kenny that my phone was clicking. It never clicked before. I hope Spindel didn't bug my phone while I was in Mexico. Pat and Peter say theirs is bugged. They run to the phone booth all the time.

Tashi pointed out a goldfinch in my garden, and a moment later three more swooped down like they were playing tag—up, down, up, around, and back! A very pretty flight pattern. He said I have red cardinals too. And hummingbirds. Chickadees. Mourning doves. Not all songbirds are dead yet.

I invited Dad to fly to Los Angeles and stay with me for a few days. He could suntan by my pool instead of Florida and sleep in my guest house. He said he'd like to. He has to make plans.

MARCH 14, 1962

Dear Red,

I'm starting to get the gist of you! Reading back through these pages, I see I've got a budding relationship with myself—a love story between me, myself, and I. And I want to go deeper. I'm the opposite of most people. My body is naked. It's my mind that is clothed. That makes writing a striptease!

MARCH 15, 1962

Dear Red,

Mary Karger surprised me with a bottle of Champagne. We drove north and swam and talked on a blanket where nobody could bug us. We stopped at Dutton's Books on the way home. When she dropped me off, I gave her a bunch of my personal letters and photographs.

She asked why and I said, "Because I trust you. You don't have to look at it. Just put it somewhere safe. I'm scared stuff is disappearing from my house." She wanted to know what makes me so paranoid. I told her, "I'm not happy with my housekeeper."

"Fire her," she said.

March 16, 1962

Dear Red,

I put on a flowered muumuu, wrapped my head in a scarf, and bought a dozen red roses. It's Grace Goddard's birthday. She died nine years ago, a suicide. I felt like being alone with her at the Westwood Memorial Park Cemetery, but it was full of little birds! As a kid I liked to grocery shop with her so we could be alone and people watch. Once we saw a father with a baby and a dog on a leash trying to make a call at the pay phone— he got so tangled up with the leash and the phone we nearly collapsed in giggles. Gee, when my dining room furniture will arrive from Mexico? I want to host a dinner party!

I can hear Santa Monica traffic in the background. The cemetery isn't a bit lonely. Aunt Grace took good care of me. I practice my deep breathing— pull the ribs up—think through the body, not along the outside of it. Shoulders float on top, free of the spine. Muscles and gravity work together. I picked up *The Thinking Body* again last night and practiced balancing my weight between the pelvis, thighs, and spine. Spinal axis is long and straight as a dinosaur's tail. Let the arms hang. That's the book I used to create Marilyn's walk way back when.

Famous people have to be like body builders, always working out because you get torn to shreds about every little imperfection. But we're all full of imperfections! That's what makes life so interesting. Kids are the best, because they don't judge people the way adults do. They're curious and spontaneous and like to play. That is how I am when I'm not working. I especially like playing with Pat and Peter's kids on the beach, even carrying baby Robin around on my hip. And I don't mind changing her diaper, feeding her, reading her books. People don't realize—I'm experienced at housekeeping! I helped out with chores when I was a kid! I know how to cook and clean, all that domestic stuff.

I need to buy art and a sofa and fix up my bedroom. In the meantime,

I'm having plush white wall-to-wall carpeting installed, everywhere but the kitchen.

MARCH 17, 1962

Dear Red,

Lunched with Joe at Bruce Wong's. When he held my hands across the table, the shutterbugs were all over us. He doesn't mind publicity, but I don't like it while I'm eating. He laughed when I claimed Irish blood—Monroe, Baker, Mortenson, Dougherty—who knows about my biological father. Of course, Italians are superior in Joe's opinion, but I couldn't convert to Italian. Arthur was amused when I converted to Judaism—he wasn't religious, only his father. I thought that if we had kids, I wanted to know which stories to tell them. Misfit. That's Arthur's word for me. If a boy on the street asks for a quarter, I give him a dollar. If he asks to shake my hand, I give him a kiss. Once when I visited an orphanage I wrote a check for $1,000, but when I saw all the kids, I tore up the check and wrote one for $10,000.

MARCH 18, 1962

Dear Red,

I was soaking in Chanel No.5 when the doorbell rang. Mrs. Murray was out, so Pat answered. She was surprised to see the general but brought him in to me. Later she asked if I love both brothers. "I don't," I said. But what if it were true? I don't believe in human ownership. Great works of art have to be shared. Dreamboat is my Sun King—I live for the day we can be together. She really didn't believe me! I had to shut her mouth with my hands. It was open so wide I could see all her fillings. I didn't want her to bite me.

March 19, 1962

Dear Red,

My friend Norman Rosten got me started writing poetry. He is a wonderful poet and has been encouraging me to write small poems since Arthur introduced us back in 1956. I showed this poem to Pat. She's a strict Catholic and says, "Marilyn, you are an education!" We spend so much time together on scripts, photo shoots, interviews, press conferences, and running around town, I forget I might shock her.

Whisked by secret service
jetted on the *Caroline*
I've zigzagged to serve my country,
Yet singing *Happy Birthday*
to Dreamboat in public
is practically an announcement!

I had my first Kundalini yoga lesson today. Ooooh, I hurt all over. We swung arms in circular motion, meditated, and chanted. Obey, serve, love, and excel—that's the yogi's mantra. We made a wish and hit our feet, thighs, hands, shoulders, and back, to stimulate the organs. Maybe spanking came from a good place, trying to turn a kid's bad mood around. Maybe. But having been hit in my life a few times, I don't think so. I was good at some of the poses, like the bow pose, which I practiced before. I grab my feet while lying on my stomach, and pull my head up— kind of like an upside-down turtle. The teacher asked if he could take a photograph of me. I said, "Sure. In a studio. Make the appointment with Pat Newcomb, my publicist."

MARCH 20, 1962

Dear Red,

Sometimes blood spoils everything, and I dread the color and pain and curse—out damn spot! Today I woke up in a thick haze. My period. My head throbbing. My insides feel like they are being raked from me in clumps. A steady bright red wound flows with nervous energy. Numb inside, shaky outside. I feel of two pieces. Turning inside out. Turning outside in. Thick tongue. Woozy head. Creepy feeling.

Weinstein gave me his daily pep talk, but he doesn't give a damn. He'll be out of a job if I misbehave. Pat asked how I felt about Jackie. I'm sure Jack and Jackie have their secrets, but his sleeping around is not one of them. And I am not one of them. Jackie and I have mutual admiration. But singing "Happy Birthday" scares me. Can twenty thousand people bite their tongue? Pat assured me that the press will not report on an affair. When she asked what I'm wearing, I said Jean Luis is designing a black high-collared dress, which is true. But I'm also having a nude dress made—Pat will know soon enough. She's coming with me.

I wake to a strange dream. A poor dark-skinned woman couldn't keep her baby in her uterus any longer—she just needed a few months more of pregnancy before the baby was viable, so I volunteered to put the baby in my uterus until it could be born. The doctor slipped the baby into me with the umbilical cord still attached to her. Suddenly, I realized I was going to be pregnant during the shooting of *Something's Got to Give*. I didn't know if I should tell Paula or not. I told the doctor to attach the umbilical cord to my vein because I had to be on the set. It would be easier to feed! I woke up laughing.

Dr. G said I was fixated on motherhood. "Fuck that," I said. "America is fixated on motherhood, and I'm not America." That shut him up. He is not used to me giving him my mind. I'm beginning to feel like I'm going in circles with him. I'm sick of him telling me what's what. I need to listen to myself.

Pat said, "Remember all the poor women begging in the market in Mexico with toddlers in their arms and pregnant bellies!"

"I think my dream was about experiencing a Frida Kahlo painting," I said.

MARCH 21, 1962

Dear Red,

I feel like a cold baked potato with catsup all over it—that's what I used to live on as a starving model. I used to get all made up to attend a half-assed party full of reefer just to get a glass of bubbly and a cracker. Money never was my goal, only developing my talent. I finally get that money is power. Liz Taylor got it long ago. Making bupkis won't do. I've got an appointment with my attorney, Rudin, to discuss a plan. Money equals respect.

Johnny Hyde died a long time ago, but he gets credit for my success. He took me in and gave me everything a woman could want, and more—things I didn't know I needed. I paid him my agent fee, but he gave me a home and put me in front of all the powerful men in Hollywood because he believed in me. He knew he wasn't wasting his time because I would never give up or throw my talent away.

MARCH 22, 1962

Dear Red,

Shit hits the fan. Dreamboat called. Photographs of me in Mexico with Fields "the communist" landed on his desk. It's hard to believe the powers that be waste their time on this kind of stuff.

I fly off to Palm Springs for the weekend. Sh'ma Yisrael. Red, I'm going to lock you in my safety deposit box so you don't disappear. No, I can't do that. I'll take you along. No, not a good idea! Gee, Maf is easier to take care of than you!

I talked to Tashi. He will design a waterproof underground hiding spot in the garden. Pronto! I'll leave you, Red, safe in the garden. We picked out a spot that can't be seen from inside the house. He'll plant some things around it. And it's spot I like to place my chair, too, so I won't attract attention if I want to write several times a day.

MARCH 23, 1962

Dear Red,

I got a tour of the set of *Something's Got to Give* and met Tippy, the dog, and the kids, Timmy and Lena. The set is a replica of George Cukor's big, beautiful house with a yard and a pool. Everyone was upbeat, but the script is still changing—a bad omen. Peter invited me to a party, but Pat's out of town, and Peter only listens when Pat says to ditch the girls. Without Pat, I don't go.

MARCH 24, 1962

Dear Red,

Andy called to invite me to his first one-man show of silkscreens, opening in November—one hundred soup cans, one hundred cola bottles, one hundred dollar bills, and me! Gee, he used the photo he took of me last time I was in New York, multiplied it, and printed it in vivid colors!

Someone asked me to tell them my secret for a washboard stomach. I said sit-ups, weight lifting, running, jump rope, yoga, and the hula hoop.

They laughed. "It's true," I said. Sometimes Pat and I work out while we plan a press conferences or a photo shoot. Movement activates the brain. Go to the zoo and watch the monkeys. They don't sit on their ass all day.

Sh'ma. I'm off to Palm Springs!

March 25, 1962

Dear Red,

Dreamboat and I were sequestered for a whole dreamy night. We slept like babes! Frank was angry because Chicky Boy didn't stay with him, especially after he built a new helicopter pad. Frankie blamed Peter, but it was White House security that nixed it. Judith Campbell was in town, too. I told Jack I saw her in LA with Giancana. He's been warned that his affairs are out of control. We have to play our cards right, he said.

I put Dreamboat on the phone with Rafe to suggest some back-strengthening exercises. Jack described his pain and got some good advice. I'm sure Rafe recognized his voice, but I never mentioned his name.

March 26, 1962

Dear Red,

Some punk at the airport saw me reading a book and said to my face, "You think that ass can get any smarter?" It's usually not strangers who insult me. I slammed my book shut and walked into the bar. The TV news showed Negros trying to register to vote. The Southern white police closed the office, but the Negros said the mayor was as racist as Hitler, and the police beat them with sticks. Their own cameraman filmed the injustice *as it happened*. I'm not a fan of TV, but getting this on the news broadcast is important.

I called Spindel from the phone booth to come and bug my house. The deed is done. I'm serious about protecting myself. My identity. The man I love. My future. I'm not going to be erased. The government can bug me. The Mafia can bug me. And I can bug myself, so I have a record too.

MARCH 27, 1962

Dear Red,

Jeane stopped by to go to dinner. "Comb your hair," she said. "You'll feel better."

What I love about going out with Jeane is that if I wear a scarf and blue jeans, strangers ask *her* for an autograph, not me, as she's in all the latest golf magazines. I didn't tell her it's the anniversary of my marriage to Arthur, six years ago today. When I think of our wedding, I remember that shutterbug from *Paris Match Magazine*, a young woman killed in a car crash in front of our Connecticut farm, trying to snap our photograph.

MARCH 28, 1962

Dear Red,

Here is an atheist poem I wrote while practicing my Swedish accent. I usually talk out loud when I write, and writing a poem has so many word choices that I get a lot of practice in.

The godfather
is not god
and fathers
are not god
even though I'd hoped so
now I know

I have to be god
if I want god

When does a girl have a true friend anyway? What's a girl to do when the powers that be, or someone I depend on, steals my words *in front of me*, in front of powerful people? *Like I'm not supposed to notice* they are ripping me off? I guess I'm still angry with Arthur.

March 29, 1962

Dear Red,

The fan club mail falls like Niagara into my lap! A lot of married men—I don't answer those. I tell the girls not to wait around to be discovered. They have to discover themselves. And don't make TV your goal. You need to be seen larger than life on the big screen. Be sure to work harder than anybody else. Be willing to make love to ten thousand men all at once, like I did in Korea. And don't forget to hang around with someone who believes in your talent.

Richard Avedon said I gave more to the camera than any other actor. All I can say is, I always give my everything!

More changes to the script were delivered tonight—yellow pages from the last changes, now pink. So much to erase in my head and memorize again. Fox is driving me crazy on purpose. I stand in the mirror memorizing for hours one way, and the next day, I memorize it another. This can't go on.

March 30, 1962

Dear Red,

I flunk. I just don't care about Dr. G's psychoanalysis any more. I'm not making progress. And these salty tears are not good for my skin. I like his kids and the family dinners. Otherwise, I feel used. He keeps talking about Anna Freud, hoping "his work," meaning my mental disorders, will impress her. Gee, I'm really stuck in the mud. Period.

March 31, 1962

Dear Red,

I made the general a Mexican omelet with fresh herbs from my garden. Out by the pool he whispered about his enemies within the government, the failed Bay of Pigs, how he didn't follow the plan laid out on his desk when he became the attorney general.

"You should be proud that you prevented another goddamn war, I said. By the way, I'm in love with your brother, and even though he can't openly love me, he loves every bit of me."

He said, "Everybody loves you, Marilyn."

"Even my enemies?" I asked.

April 1, 1962

Dear Red,

Paula arrives from New York tomorrow. She's my second set of eyes to make sure I'm Ellen Arden, lost wife pulling a Swedish nanny trick to get *my* house, *my* kids, and *my* husband back. The storyline is that I was stranded for five years on an island with a big, handsome castaway, so I find a homely shoe salesman to pose instead. I don't give a shit if Paula infuriates everyone around me. And the script—they're still pulling the rug out from under me with the rewrites. Like a cartoon, they want me to fall on my ass so they can laugh.

I once had a coach named Natasha. I met her at Columbia Pictures and stayed with her for about seven years. I moved in with Natasha and her daughter for a few months in the early '50s. Somehow, when life is hard, it's easier to have a close circle of women to rely on. I read that even in Hitler's death camps, women formed small circles to help stay sane. If one was sick or pregnant, they would steal or do anything to protect her. But someone started a rumor that Natasha and I were lovers. Why? Two adult women can't live together without being called lesbians? I say to hell with what people think. Natasha had an irritating jealous streak, even when I went out for the afternoon with her daughter, let alone on dates or to parties. And I said to someone once that she was jealous, like a husband. Maybe the word *husband* started the rumor. Jealousy is about ownership, and I don't believe in owning people. I refused to defend myself or convince the world that it wasn't true. I learned a long time ago to never fight the rumors. It'll drain the blood out of you.

Cheryl Crawford introduced me to the Strasbergs in New York in 1954, and I fell in love with the method. That's when I sent Natasha a memo telling her that I had gotten involved with the Actors Studio, and I wouldn't need her services any more. People criticized me and said it wasn't a proper ending to a long working relationship. No good-bye ever is.

APRIL 2, 1962

Dear Red,

Maf breathes. I breathe. We breathe. He's sleeps. He wheezes. We breathe together. I end up panting. I take a deep breath. I take off my eye mask, pull back the blackout curtains, and look at starry sky. Dr. G warned me he is leaving for Europe soon to meet with Anna Freud. He's nervous. I'm nervous. But he doesn't say exactly when he's leaving. Joan, his adorable teenage daughter, promises she'll stop by with her stack of forty-fives so we can twist and shout.

Paula can sleep at my house, he says, but Paula retreats to her hotel as soon as filming is over. She likes to order from room service. No roast to cook. She can read. Talk on the phone. Have privacy. I invited Paula's daughter Susie to visit. She is living in San Francisco now and has some films coming up. And a boyfriend. I haven't seen her since last year.

Pat Lawford came over. We went for a drive along Mulholland and ended up at the Santa Monica pier watching the lights of the Ferris wheel go round in the black sky, listening to the cold, dark waves lap the pilings. Rafe came around midnight. He knows my body better than anyone. He starts with my head, my forehead, my jaw. Most important is my neck and back and tush. Slowly he moves down each of my legs. Massages my feet, my toes. So lovingly. Turns me over and massages my arms. Like me, Rafe believes in the underdog. Maf, you hear that? No, you're asleep. I met him at one of Paula and Lee's parties when he was still acting.

Gee, I wish I could sleep. Sheep—1,001, 1,002, 1,003, 1,004, 1,005, 1,006, 1,007, 1,008, 1,009, 1,010 … 12,305. My mind won't go slow, like it's jinxed by the edge, afraid of falling off to sleep like sleep is a dangerous cliff. Jittery, tense muscles, the curse at the end of the day. Fear of ending it. Fear of making the leap. The fear of not sleeping. The fear that if I don't sleep, I can't be my best.

Instead, after a day at the studio, I'm beat and ready for sleep. I take a nap. I eat in bed. I make phone calls in bed. I read in bed. I listen to records. I listen to the radio. I write in my diary. I make to-do lists in bed. I memorize my lines. *All in bed.*

Sometimes when my mind won't turn off, I pull aside my blackout curtain and try to recite the big wheel of nature. It's a totally exhausting job, naming everything from the big, fiery beginning, the formation of galaxies with suns, planets and moons and comets and the gasses and heat, oxygen and carbon and water, minerals, soil, temperature and seasons with earth tilting and orbiting, back and forth through the seasons, and things like magnets and gravity, volcanoes, earthquakes, tides, waves, hurricanes, tornadoes, typhoons, droughts, snow, hail, rain, fog, wind, mountains, deserts, jungles, continents, houses, cities, farms, suburbs, birds, trees, tree houses, plants, crops, grass, flowers, fruit, grain, animals, earthworms, fish, whales, sea lions, jellyfish, microscopic stuff, algae, mushrooms, cars, people, paintings, sculpture, music, language, dinosaur bones, and all the African villages and rivers, ancient cultures and pyramids, and China and India and Japan, and all the countries of the world, on and on until I end up with my purse—wallet, photos, money, checkbook, pen, note cards, driver's license, SAG card, pills, compact, tissues, lipstick, scarf, keys, gum, sunglasses. Everything has to be remembered before I can sleep. If I'm cranky, I get impatient and self-critical and come up with another more interesting exercise, like singing all the songs I've recorded or reciting the entire film I'm working on. I torture myself, when other human beings can just turn out the light.

APRIL 3, 1962

Dear Red,

Dreamboat promised to sneak me into the Lincoln Bedroom when he made it to the White House, and it wasn't long after he was sworn in that I got my call. A car picked me up, and I was swept into an elevator to the second floor of the West Wing. It was beautiful! I touched the golden sofa, the desk with the Gettysburg Address, and the rosewood bed with a canopy shaped like a crown of purple satin. He came in past midnight and popped champagne, and I slipped into nothing. After we made love, he fell into a deep sleep and I stayed awake all night, hoping to seduce Lincoln's ghost.

I promised myself I would write the facts of life in my diary. Otherwise no one will read it. Pat says people like to read what others write when it's the truth, but when it comes to storytelling, I know character and plot help pull the reader along. Gee, now that I think about it, did she mean the facts of my life or the facts of life? I've switched the facts of my life to create drama so many times no one knows the real me. So, here's the truth: Botticelli is my inspiration. You shouldn't marry the boy next door when you're still a kid. I never told a shrink that I'm nearly deaf in my right ear—some things are just too personal. I met Frank Sinatra when I was sixteen, just a kid, and his voice got into my head, permanently! I've listened to him every day for almost twenty years. We've gone through times of taking each other seriously—we lay on, then we lay off. In fact, my first orgasm happened by accident when I was learning to sing. So for me, singing and sex are the same big sweet spot.

April 4, 1962

Dear Red,

Paula says it's the coffee that's giving me sleep problems. I'm going to research the effects. Just one more addiction. Human beings aren't perfect. Lee agrees. He says, "Darling, I see no reason to hide what's inside you. Problems and being human go hand-in-hand. I am not the church." Well I'm not the church either. Only, now I have to sneak coffee. Maybe she is really objecting to what I pour into my coffee. So why doesn't she say that then?

Breakfast: grapefruit, black coffee
Lunch: caviar, crackers, bloody Mary
Dinner: cottage cheese, hard-boiled egg, raw carrots, bubbly

April 5, 1962

Dear Red,

Norman sent me his new spring poem. I called him and read my haiku reply three times. I had to omit the word *like* at the beginning of the second line, I said, because of the seven-syllable limit. He said he likes the verb action and suggested that I gather a collection of my poems into a book. He'll write an introduction.

The cherry tree pops
a merry-go-round pink bob,
and waves: toodle-loo!

Norman reads poems like tea leaves. He said the words *pops* and *bob* on the first level conjure images of popsicles and a hairdo, but what you really mean, Marilyn, is action. The verbs: *pops*, as in blossoms bursting open; *bob*, as a dodging, bouncing movement. The pink tree in full bloom sways back and forth in the breeze. *Waves*, another verb, is also the custom of moving one's hand rather than using words to say good-bye as the blossoms blow away. So it is the cycle of life with a positive spin. He said I should call it Cherry Pops. A poem is a treat. He wants me to title them. He says this poem is very Marilyn. Sexually sophisticated and childlike at the same time. "You know not what you do," he said, "but you do it well."

Here is another poem I'm working on. I'd like to make it longer because I believe a good kiss can last a lifetime, but I haven't gotten to that line yet.

Small talk rubs
me wrong lips
speak much longer
Just kiss

APRIL 6, 1962

Dear Red,

Ellen Arden says to the dog, "What on earth have they been feeding you, you silly old thing! Tippy wouldn't try to bite me, would you, Tippy?" To the kids, she says, "You don't remember me, do you? Would you like me to stay? You know what? You two kids are my two best sweethearts in the whole world!" When I got home, I called my stepchildren, Joe Jr., and Jane and Robert Miller because they are mine—and they deserve all the love I can give them.

Breakfast: water, black coffee, water
Lunch: watermelon juice, water, melon
Dinner: bubbly, bubbly, three crackers, and crab

APRIL 7, 1962

Dear Red,

I found my best teachers on stage. Like Lily St. Cyr—I copied her makeup, the way she dressed, her striptease. She was Ted Jordan's girlfriend, a first-class artist and all I had to pay was a couple bucks cover charge to get educated. Now look at me. I pay a hairdresser, makeup artist, multiple yoga instructors, publicist, coach, doctors, massage therapist, dressmakers, business manager, maid in New York, housekeeper, lawyers …

As promised, I finally got around to writing my biography for Dreamboat. It's just a partial list. How could I ever make a full list? That's the thing about lists—there are plenty of blank spaces between the lines.

I was born at LA General.
My mother was abandoned by her husband.
When I was twelve days old, Mother paid Aunt Ida to take care of me in

Hawthorne, California—Grandma Della lived across the street and had me baptized by Sister Aimee.

At six I was sexually molested by Aunt Ida's boarder.

At nine my puppy was shot dead by a neighbor.

I moved in with Mother, but that lasted only seven months.

I moved in with Aunt Grace, Doc, and Beebe.

I dropped out of high school at sixteen to marry Jimmy.

Met Bob Mitchum and Frank Sinatra.

Jimmy went to war.

I learned to drive a stick and got a job at the Radio Plane Company.

A photographer named Conover took pictures of girls working at the factory.

I signed with Emmeline Snively at Blue Book Modeling Agency.

My photograph landed on the covers of magazines.

Was introduced to Helen Ainsworth.

Met Ben Lyon at Twentieth Century Fox.

First motion picture screen test.

Changed my name to Marilyn Monroe.

Divorced Jimmy.

Moved in with Mother and Aunt Ana.

Met Freddy Karger, fell in love, and learned to sing.

Met Johnny Hyde and made two films.

Signed six-month contract with Columbia Pictures.

Signed with Twentieth Century Fox.

Fell in love with Dreamboat.

Married and divorced Joe DiMaggio.

Worked with coach Natasha Lytess six years.

Formed Marilyn Monroe Productions.

Worked with Lee and Paula Strasberg.

Converted to Judaism and married Arthur Miller.

Backed him during the House Un-American Activities Committee hearings.

Divorced Arthur Miller.

Bought Brentwood House.

April 8, 1962

Dear Red,

Mrs. Murray said, "Marilyn, you can rely on me while Dr. Greenson is on vacation."

When I looked at her, all I saw were her spooky dark carved nostrils. "Rely on you for what?" I asked.

"If you feel the need to talk, I can help you relax."

"No, Mrs. Murray. Our agreement is that you are here to clean my house, fill my refrigerator, and drive me on errands."

I heard Lee's voice instructing me on how to react to Mrs. Murray: the character feels like screaming, but by remaining silent, staring directly into the maniac's eyes, the character retains the power. Whatever you have to say must be said with your facial expression and body language as you walk away. So here is what my walk says: Mrs. Murray, you will never be my savior. I agree that screaming this would be giving her what she wants—an excuse to call Dr. G to inform him I'm having a tantrum, triggering Dr. E's arrival with a sedative.

April 9, 1962

Dear Red,

Ellen Arden says to Wally's character, the shoe salesman, "Would you have lunch with me? I'd be so grateful if you'd take it out. My foot's grown! Go barefoot for five years and look what happens!" Ellen says to Dean Martin, her husband, "I was afraid you'd misunderstand about that. Would it make any difference if I knew him? How long does it take to tell a woman your wife is back? See? I just said it. It takes two seconds, but it's been two days."

APRIL 10, 1962

Dear Red,

First day of shooting. Paula said I was in perfect form—I felt it. But where was Cukor? I've never experienced the director not bothering to show up on the first day. How disrespectful is that? When I got home, I found Mrs. Murray had packed up and left. When the fridge was bare yesterday, I told her she was a lazy housekeeper, to quit snooping, and to stay out of my room.

I was liberated. I danced, sang, and lit a fire in the hibachi out by the pool, and listened to music. The stars came out. I pulled the phone cord out there and made a bunch of calls, first on the East Coast, and when it got too late, the West Coast. Now it's 4:00 a.m. and I haven't slept a wink. Can't.

APRIL 11, 1962

Dear Red,

Sick Bad Shit Fucked Day. Love, love, love
you, Red. Be here for me. Be here. Hear me.
Can't write. Marilyn

APRIL 12, 1962

Dear Red,

Weinstein, my producer and babysitter, not my doctor, called it an OD. Too many pills, he said, but I counted them! I know what I'm doing. Everyone in Hollywood has their formula for counting pills. He says he found me unconscious. Well, I was up all night and *was just blissfully finally*

sleeping. I missed a meeting at Fox, he said. "I'm going to tell them you had
a heart attack." Then Weinstein called my secretary and told her to call
Mrs. Murray and offer her a raise to come back. I'm totally humiliated.

APRIL 13, 1962

Dear Red,

Fox threw Liz a *queen size* thirtieth birthday party. Of course, the article
didn't report that Fox is going broke, or that Fox is pressuring *Marilyn*
into slave labor to save their ass. Still, I am the biggest hit at the box office
for the last decade, as Joe, and Dad, and Pat Lawford, and Pat Newcomb,
and the president of the United States remind me every time I speak to
them. The tiger's going to stop purring and *roar*. Pat's on her way over.
Hedda Hopper's piece in the *Chicago Tribune* still stings: "Can Marilyn
Ever Be Happy?"

That is so pathetic.

APRIL 14, 1962

Dear Red,

Sh'ma. Paula and I are heading to New York for a week. The film has
been postponed due to problems with the script, not because of me. By
the way, it occurred to me that my well-meaning Aunt Ida, banging on
the bedroom door in her baggy housedress, telling me and the boy they
called my twin that we were going to burn in hell if I didn't open up—this
is probably the root of my recurring nightmare of smoke seeping from
beneath the closet door!

"Darling," Lee said, "you want to be remembered for the work: the best actors and actresses don't necessarily have the biggest fan clubs." That brought me down to my knees.

APRIL 15, 1962

Dear Red,

I met Milton and Amy for dinner to discuss The Marilyn Monroe Shakespeare Company—our dream from long ago. It burns inside me again. Milton is not the perfect partner, and God knows, I'm not either, but we had a good brainstorm about who I could tap. There are plenty of possibilities. Not a creative partner, but a financial partner.

Walking down the street, I remembered Yoshiko. I danced with her when Jimmy was away at war. She hid in a cellar during the Japanese roundup and after the war, never felt safe. A girl at the Radio Airplane factory introduced us. I climbed down a ladder into her clean, sparse underground room. She painted my face white and dressed me in traditional Japanese clothing. I mimed her movements. She didn't speak English, but she said so much.

Truth tilts sideways
From outer galaxies
Through the ages landing
In a sublime place
of pleasure and pain

APRIL 16, 1962

Dear Red,

Arthur and I married in 1956, and our honeymoon started in London with the filming of *The Prince and the Showgirl*. The day we had tea with the Queen we had our first fight. I saw that he copied everything I said into his diary! Olivier and Vivian Leigh squeezed into the car with us. We all had practiced our bows, walking backward, and the proper titles, but I was the only one who knew my cues perfectly. Arthur tripped, Lawrence didn't bow, and his wife bowed multiple times. Things went downhill from there. Paula had a breakdown and flew back to New York. Lee was scheduled to take her place, but we asked Arthur's best friend, Norman Rosten's wife, Hedda, to step in instead. She could nurture us both. After that fiasco, I was pregnant and Arthur and I rented a cottage in Amagansett. It was fall, and dreamy quiet, and beautiful. We were absolutely alone and happy, until the miscarriage.

April 17, 1962

Dear Red,

Paula tells Lee what I say. He repeats it back to me. And I pay them! Oh well, some people say they treat me better than their own daughter, Susie. She looked like Liz in *National Velvet* when she played Anne Frank on Broadway. It's hard to understand why Lee refused to coach Susie, and when she asked me, I couldn't come up with a good explanation. Now, I see Lee as a human being, not the god I thought he was. Life is not a cherry tree.

April 18, 1962

Dear Red,

Oops! My fingers were in Dreamboat's hair, my legs around his, when a secret serviceman burst into the room. Jackie is threatening a divorce over the birthday plans. Luckily, Joe Kennedy is stepping in to make her a substantial gift. "Chin up," Dreamboat said. "We're champions at making the most of each and every moment." Gee, Rev. King sent Jack a beautiful

130-page letter. He said, "Legislation can't change the heart, but it can restrain the heartless."

April 19, 1962

Dear Red,

Shit! I'm in bed with a box of tissues. I caught Lee's flu. Paula soothes me with Yiddish sayings like a soft tongue breaks the bones—she's earning her five thousand this week by making me chicken soup. She mentioned Susie in San Francisco trying out free love and laments the fact that her daughter never had a real childhood—she grew up too quickly. Paula worries about Johnny, too, sitting by his father's side at the studio, without any encouragement from Lee.

April 20, 1962

Dear Red,

Weinstein yelled at me. He said, "Jesus, Marilyn, don't you have any Kotex?" I was dripping blood all over my bathrobe, the chair, and the white carpet while he and the new scriptwriter, Walter Burnstein, sat in my living room, poring over *Something's Got to Give*. Nunnally was fired because he and Weinstein didn't get along! I pulled my claws out and whipped my tail around, glad to be trailing blood. Weinstein was shocked to see my list of demands. I'm still blowing my nose, but I know what I want.

April 21, 1962

Dear Red,

I was thinking about the shitty job Dr. Cottrell did stitching up my gallbladder surgery. It took me a year of fighting depression before I finally accepted that scar. But imagine what veterans face. Dreamboat suffers from constant back pain, and he lost his brother to the war. I'm happy he doesn't need to take care of me financially, geographically, socially, or historically, so being together is like being kids again.

Dread head bed
Ouch couch grouch
Bitch ditch itch
Suck luck fuck

I took two more pills—that makes seven—and finished the Champagne I started at sunset with Pat out by the pool. We brainstormed ways to cash in on Marilyn. You've got the right word. Cash. "Money equals power," I said. Look what I let happen. I made $50 off Tom Kelley's nude. Tom Kelley made $500. John Baumgarth made $750,000.

Luxine was a beautiful girl in my grade school. I wonder what ever happened to her. Probably at the pinnacle of success as June Lockhart, suburban stay-at-home mom—that was what a girl could hope for back then. Norma Jeane, human bean. Human being. Human being. Human being. Being human. Being. Bingo.

APRIL 22, 1962

Dear Red,

Fuck. I'm too sick to begin filming. Dr. E. says filming should be postponed for a month. Even Fox's new doctor agrees. But Fox said insurance won't cover it. No shit. They are blaming it on me, a cover-up for their problems. Well, I won't film unless I feel 100 percent because I have to be my best. None of them have to perform like I do. Film is forever! Joe sent me beautiful white Easter lilies. When I told him I wasn't feeling well, he said he'd stop by.

Breakfast: black coffee, water
Lunch: water, water, water
Dinner: chicken soup with ginger, peas, and carrots

APRIL 23, 1962

Dear Red,

Dr. E treated my viral infection. Paula helped me through the day with little nips of vodka. Everyone was happy. My stand-in, Evelyn Moriarty, is sweet. Agnes, Fox's hairdresser, is everyone's mama. She said, "Marilyn, you're a lucky girl to have such thick hair." It's good to remember hair isn't one of my problems! Joe came over for an hour. It was warm enough to sit outside and have a private conversation. I told him about the problems on the set. He's adamant that I speak with his attorney. I respect his business sense, and he cares about me, but I have to remember, he is not my knight in shining armor. We tried that myth, and it doesn't work.

Breakfast: grapefruit, black coffee
Lunch: cheese sandwich, black coffee
Dinner: tuna steak, bubbly

APRIL 24, 1962

Dear Red,

Imagine a close-up of me today. My acute sinusitis would frighten the audience. I can't even get out of bed. Besides, I refuse to meet the shah of Iran. He and his wife are visiting the set today. He doesn't recognize Israel, so let Ginger Rogers and Bob Hope entertain them. I met Khrushchev years ago, but I don't feel like playing the Hollywood celebrity-meets-politician game anymore. I've got private meetings with the only one who counts.

APRIL 25, 1962

Dear Red,

I called in sick again. It's documented by three doctors, including Fox's own Dr. Segal. It's bad for me, so much pressure from Fox. It's in my chest. I can hardly breathe. I know what my body can and cannot do. There are two ways to look at myself: victim of the press, or resister. The way I feel is real. What everyone else says I feel is not real.

Rereading you, Red—I see that I'm stronger when I'm alone. I don't have to expend energy on others, just me. Being lonely is sad. Being me, alone at home, alone with you, is powerful.

APRIL 26, 1962

Dear Red,

"A fool's mouth is his destruction," says Paula, "and his lips are the snare of his soul. Just focus on me." But I tell her everything depends on Ellen Arden, her unspoken and precise reality. The way van Gogh paints his shoes, no one could mistake them for their own. "Reality is not conventional," says Lee, "and just because you hear action, it doesn't mean you have to move, darling." Real drama is like water, a reflection. I don't believe any water is ever still. My heart is beating! I'm breathing! I want my audience to know I am alive!

Black coffee
Dark chocolate pudding
Grapefruit juice
Black coffee
Caviar and crackers
Raw oysters
Champagne
Bubble bath

APRIL 27, 1962

Dear Red,

Agnes called to check up on me. They're shooting the bedroom scene with
Dean Martin and Cyd Charisse. Everyone's telling me that Cyd is padding
her bra. Maybe she had implant surgery? When I asked Weinstein, he
said, "Why do you care? You're the star, Marilyn. All anyone wants to
look at is you."

Mrs. Murray drove me downtown in her beautiful green jalopy. I asked
her if I could buy it from her. She didn't answer. I love it because when I'm
driving it or riding in it, no one notices me. I picked out a birthday present
for Dreamboat, a handsome gold watch, and asked to have it engraved.

APRIL 28, 1962

Dear Red,

I think of Timmy and Lena on the set, and tears roll down my cheeks.
They are about the ages of the children Arthur and I would have had if I
hadn't miscarried, twice. I was absolutely starving this afternoon. I broke
my vow and ate a hamburger. Now it's mooing inside me. Once humans
stop killing animals, they'll learn how to stop killing each other. I'm going
to stick my finger down my throat.

APRIL 29, 1962

Dear Red,

All I wanted to do when I got home was take a nap, and there was Mrs.
Murray, snooping around in my room—again! It put me over the edge.
I was out of control screaming, so she did her usual—called Dr. G and

waited for him on the driveway. Dr. E arrived and gave me his usual—vitamins mixed with XYZ and whatever. On lighter note, Dad wants to take me to the Seattle World's Fair. An exhibit called the Bubbleator explains the history of the world, from the Acropolis to Marilyn Monroe!

I fell asleep from seven until eleven and woke up loving my empty house. I locked all the doors and windows and wandered around. Sometime I don't want to tell people the truth because the person I'm talking to doesn't deserve to know what I'm thinking, and then suddenly my ears are burning because I hear myself spitting out some other truth I hadn't even realized. For example, a few months ago I met a friend for lunch and was complaining to her about being treated unprofessionally by Fox, that I really don't feel I owe Fox anything, so I was short and to the point, avoiding all the gossipy details she wanted to know, and I realized that what I said about Fox was exactly the way I felt about her! What a strange day. Next time she calls, I'll decline the lunch invitation.

Dreamboat's mantra: It's not what you are, it's what people think you are that causes the trouble.

April 30, 1962

Dear Red,

My dress is absolutely beautiful! Jean Louis has eighteen seamstresses sewing beads in strategic places, to hide pubic hair and nipples. The plan is to sew me into it at the last minute. I'll need to be carried down a flight of stairs. Meanwhile I'm working with Lionel Newman on the song and writing a surprise stanza ... to thank Mr. President.

Hap-py birth-day *to* you
Hap-py birth-*day* to you
Hap-py *birth*-day Mis-ter Pres-i-dent
Hap-py birth-day to *you.*

MAY 1, 1962

Dear Red,

I played volleyball on the beach at Lawfords until Dreamboat arrived. We slipped away for private time, but Peter interrupted with a camera, snapping photographs of us in a bubble bath! Pat told me stories of growing up in their big family. Christmas on the Riviera, living in Britain while her father was an ambassador, dating McCarthy as a teen, of all men! When her father endorsed Hitler, that was the end of her parents' happy marriage.

Jack interrupted: "I was the only one who stood up to Mother—I was deliberately messy and late just to make her mad."

"Where did she spend time?" I asked.

"Touring the National Parks, spas, and visiting friends."

Pat chimed in: "Mother taught the girls to be independent."

Jack said, "Father was the boys' nurturing parent."

Pat smiled. "You were the rebel," she said and wrapped her arm around him. She said, "But I still think it will be one of the girls who make the biggest mark on humanity!"

Jack smiled. "We'll see," he said, and whisked me onto the dance floor. That was a rare event. He whispered that he's on new pain medication. A sweet end to the evening!

MAY 2, 1962

Dear Red,

Three of us from Dennison's party went to the beach with Timothy Leary. We swallowed a tiny square of yellow paper with a drop of LSD. The day was a blurry kaleidoscope of bumblebee eyes. We were like fleas in the sand. A grand old bearded man winked at me from the sky! I laughed so hard my face froze in a smile. When I got home, my mouth and lips and teeth all seemed kind of grotesque and fascinating in the mirror. I was dehydrated and exhausted too! Dr. Leary thinks our mind is open at birth but closes as life's habits replace actual experience.

MAY 3, 1962

Dear Red,

Skolsky sent the first draft of the Jean Harlow story for comments. He is aiming to start filming this fall. Mother and Aunt Grace were determined to teach me everything about Harlow—where she grew up, her films, her hairstyles. When she died, they drove me by her husband's houses, and we paid our respects at the cemetery. All her gravestone said was "The Baby."

My nickname
Zelda Zonk
ZZ like MM
Parallel lines
Parallel lives
Me inside me
Lives inside lines

May 4, 1962

Dear Red,

Dreamboat was alone on our good night call. I told him about the Timothy Leary trip, the Jean Harlow script, and how Maf chased a porcupine up a tree!

"Marilyn," he said, "you are my cornucopia."

"Yes," I said, "fruity!"

"No," he argued, "an abundance of sweetness and a good heart. One day you'll be a good addition to the family."

"You needn't flatter me," I said.

"No, no, I'm speaking the truth," he insisted. "Dad loves you."

"But he hasn't met me," I said with a pout. Then I added: "I know, our day will come."

May 5, 1962

Dear Red,

Pat is out of town today, so I skipped my exercise routine. Once in a while I take a day off, though I may work out later. I attacked the stack of books next to my bed. Norman sent me the poem called "This is Just to Say" by WCW, a doctor poet in New Jersey. I like the way he loves his wife without ever mentioning her, and how you can sense peace and quiet of the house. Wait a sec, I just reread the poem from the wife's point of view: he ate *her* plums. I don't feel peace from him after all. I feel his controlling chill.

May 6, 1962

Dear Red,

Dad isn't feeling well. I'm concerned. He's seventy-seven and lost ten pounds. It's his stomach. He can't eat. He said, "Maybe it's a little cancer."

I said, "But maybe … it's … just … a … little … ulcer."

He laughed. I asked what was so funny. He said, "It's your delivery, Marilyn. Only you could turn that line into comedy." Gee, Dad, I'm happy to hear you laugh!

Jeanne stopped by this afternoon. I don't see her much, not like we used to. We sat around the pool, flipping through magazines. We got into a laughing fit remembering escapades back in New York on blind double dates. Some men thought one blond was as dumb as two, but boy did we give them the runaround! We were real goofs with a lot of tricks up our sleeves!

May 7, 1962

Dear Red,

Agnes said I passed out under the hair dryer at 6:00 a.m. The new Fox doctor brought me around with smelling salts and sent me home. Dreamboat called with very private information—he receives more inheritance on his forty-fifth birthday and will save it for our future! I had to hide my Mona Lisa smile because my house is full of people pacing between my bedroom and living room—Weinstein, Mrs. Murray, Dr. G, Paula, and Pat—and all I want to do is close my eyes and dream.

May 8, 1962

Dear Red,

Weinstein doesn't get it. He called me three times today to ask my temperature. How am I supposed to get any rest? I remembered the cartoon about the elephant sitting on the mouse's tail, and finally I said to him, "Get Fox's big *ass* off *my* tail! That means you. Don't call!" I didn't eat anything all day, only black coffee and fresh-squeezed orange juice, and one of Mrs. Lindberg's brewer's yeast drinks for lunch. This afternoon I had eight glasses of water. Mrs. Lindberg swears that eight glasses a day is essential. By the way, cold water is quite delicious, and filling!

May 9, 1962

Dear Red,

The mirror doesn't lie: a woman's face is alluring, but breasts are the most sensuous part of a female body. Gravity hasn't gotten mine yet—thanks to my routine of fifty pushups a day and forty minutes of weightlifting. Someone at Dennison's party said that women are the only mammals to have breasts from puberty through adult life. Can you imagine that? He credited breasts as the factor in human evolution! As a kid, I got my mouth taped shut for asking Aunt Ida how she got her breasts. As an adult, the taboo subjects are sex, religion, money, politics, and people, especially if they are in the room.

May 10, 1962

Dear Red,

Fox sent a telegram stating that I was required to show up for the shoot tomorrow. Screw them! I called Rudin to reply that I am sick and reminded them that I will be out May 17 and 18 for the president's birthday at Madison Square Garden. Cukor called and said that the film is five days behind schedule and ordered me not to attend the birthday party. I said I got written permission from Weinstein two months ago, and if that's not enough, the president of the United States said he'd write me an excuse, if necessary.

May 11, 1962

Dear Red,

Gee, when I finish this film with Fox, I'll have only one last film and I'll be free to pursue some serious artistic roles waiting for me. And the Marilyn Monroe Shakespeare Company. I can hardly wait to see that curtain rise, featuring the most talented misfits in the world!

May 12, 1962

Dear Red,

It is raining today, so unusual in Los Angeles this time of year. Pat and I went on some errands— I had to pick up the jewelry I'm borrowing for the birthday party and stop by for a last fitting of my dress. Pat's eyes about rolled out of her head when she saw the dress! Jean Louis was pleased and is sending his top seamstresses to New York for final touches. On the way home, a wind came up from the Pacific and uprooted palm trees along Santa Monica, nearly overturning Pat's car! I'm already saying my Sh'ma in preparation for flying.

MAY 13, 1962

Dear Red,

Dad called to hear me sing our usual Sunday night "Happy Birthday" lullaby one last time. He wanted to know logistics. I told him Jack is sitting in the first row, twelve feet from the stage. He is seated a few rows above with Pat and Bobby and Ethel. Jack's parents will be on the aisle a few seats over. As much as I would like to, it may not be appropriate for me to meet Rose and Joseph, I'm told. I'm the last of a dozen performers—I go with the cake, of course.

MAY 14, 1962

Dear Red,

I'm exhausted. The dog trainer couldn't get Tippy to bark and yelled at him all day long. Tippy loves me but wouldn't obey for the camera, only in rehearsals. We were all so frustrated, all except Dean, who happily swung his golf club like a pendulum back and forth, oblivious of time passing. Tippy ran the show. Cukor can't blame me for today's problems. In the end, even *he* was yelling at poor Tippy!

Skolsky called to tell me Jackie entertained Arthur Miller and his new wife, Inge Morath, at the White House. Arthur was seated next to Jackie, and she asked a lot of questions about the *Misfits*, and if Roslyn was modeled after Marilyn Monroe. So when I called tonight, before she passed the phone to Jack, I let her know that I plan to marry the president one day. She gave a little chuckle and said I was charming. I wonder, did she think I was joking? Or maybe she thought I could be right! "Who do you want to marry?" I asked.

May 15, 1962

Dear Red,

The general said that violence is the result of people who don't have an opportunity to express their culture artistically. Museums are important to education—be sure to take note of what's missing. He offered to give me a personal tour of the Chinese art collection at the Metropolitan Museum next time I'm in New York. "Do you explore cemeteries?" I asked. "It's a favorite pastime of mine. They're quite beautiful on a sunny day, and death is *the* great equalizer."

May 16, 1962

Dear Red,

Every day the script changes, and every night a new draft arrives on my doorstep for me to memorize—and now the new changes are slipped in on the original white paper, as if it isn't really a change. It's dizzy merry-go-round I can't get off! No wonder I can't remember my lines. Cukor and Weinstein are spreading rumors that I'm crazy. But I'm sane! I'm singing. I'm happy.

Hap-py birth-day *to* you
Hap-py birth-*day* to you
Hap-py *bithday*-day Mis-ter Pres-i-dent
Hap-py birth-day to *you*.

May 17, 1962

Dear Red,

Sh'ma. Peter, Pat, and I flew by helicopter from Fox Studio to LA airport to New York. Dad is flying in from Florida. Twenty thousand people are invited. Gee, that's a big audience. "Darling," Lee says. "You are the champion of the private moment in public. You are Houdini with the cat exercise. You can make twenty thousand loins throb and embarrass them at the same time."

I've prepared my song, separating breath from vowel and consonant. My happy theatrical sounds round into an overall sensation. Yes, *I'm the song*. I'm the gestures of a Greek sculpture in a silky dress of flesh.

I'm looking forward to spending time in my New York apartment. I feel safe in New York. Less stressed. New York is home and a vacation at the same time. In New York it is easier to feel a part of humanity. In New York I'm more hopeful. In New York, I feel like people have their thinking caps on.

May 18, 1962

Dear Red,

I dined with Hedda and Norman in Brooklyn Heights. Hedda made brisket, potatoes, and baked Alaska. I took one bite of each. Patricia held my hand and sang out the fruit streets—Pineapple, Orange, Cranberry—on our evening walk, purposefully steering clear of Arthur's block on Montague Street. The bomb dropped when I got back to my apartment. A telegram from Twentieth Century Fox: Due to failure to work, Marilyn Monroe is in breach of contract and dire consequences will follow. I telephoned Dreamboat and reminded him I'm doing my patriotic duty. He said he would see what he can do, not to worry, get some shut-eye. I called Rudin. Dad. My ex-ex. Everywhere I look, I see a mushroom cloud.

May 19, 1962

Dear Red,

Today is sweetie's big day. I woke up fresh, past noon. I took care of me and had a long, warm bath with Chanel No. 5. Jack and Bobby will take care of Fox. I'm humming "Happy Birthday" in all kinds of jazz tempos. Relax and concentrate. I practiced eight hours yesterday with my accompanist Hank Jones— that was for sixteen bars of music! We're ripe. Whitey will be here in a few to do my makeup. I've decided to darken the mole above my lip.

May 20, 1962

Dear Red

At the last minute, Bobby wanted his hairdresser, Mickey Song, to comb out my hair. I didn't feel like anyone new touching me tonight, I said. Bobby sat me down and snapped his fingers to get my attention.

"Marilyn," he said, "I've shown Mickey the style you want with the flip on one side. I owe him a favor—this will make his career."

I said, "But he already does Eva Gabor, and Frankie and Rachel Welch."

"He is family," Bobby said. And then I felt what Pat Lawford had so many times before. I threw up my arms: but only one photograph, and find me a cracker. I needed to eat something before I fainted.

I remember the drumroll like thunder, and Peter's announcement: "Ladies and gentleman, the *late* Marilyn Monroe!" I dumped my white stole in his arms and wagged my tail. A sudden hush. I had to shield my eyes to see Dreamboat. He smiled. I picked up the microphone. I hesitated. I started talking the lines, like I was afraid of my own voice. Then I poured it on, and I boiled over. After the birthday song came, "Thanks for the Memory," and the words I wrote:

Thanks, Mr. President,
For all the things you've done,
The battles you've won,
The way you deal with US steel,
And our problems by the ton,
We thank you—so much.

Then, it was back to "Happy Birthday." "Come on, everybody! All together now!" I yelled, jumping on the downbeat. Twenty thousand people joined in. It was redemptive. Four strong men carried in a gigantic birthday cake, and Dreamboat joined me on stage.

One of the happiest moments of my life took place backstage—I introduced Jack to Dad: the love of my life and my dad. It was such a common, plain old happy moment. At the afterparty Dad was tired, and I was a little worried and wouldn't leave his side. I made sure he sat down and ate a sandwich and had something to drink. Diahann Carroll performed. It was chilling and calming. I was grateful to cool down. The general and Jack and I chatted a bit. Some photographers got in, and the general was livid as they snapped away. Bobby smashed one of their cameras. They *loved* my performance. And my dress, I might add. My natural shape. They assured me Fox wouldn't fire me after this. I took Daddy to his hotel and later met Dreamboat at the Carlyle. I had to switch to my stiff, ugly stenographer's outfit—black wig, steno pad in hand, loafers, escorts, the whole bit. Of course, it's always fun taking it off for him.

Later we snuggled in our bathrobes, his arm tucked around my waist. I said I was sorry that Jackie didn't come to the party, and isn't it ironic that Jackie chases real live foxes on a horse while I'm wrangling Twentieth Century Fox!

'Therein lies the difference," he said. "Jackie is a woman of the world, and you are a woman in the world."

"Only two little words different," I said with a smile.

"Little words count, Marilyn." He pulled away to look at me. "I suggest you read *Elements of Style*, a brilliant little book on little words."

"Gee," I said, "I guess you can't say man of the moon. It has to be man in the moon."

He suddenly had a big smile. "The man in the moon is the one that's eternal."

Then he tore the white satin paper off his birthday gift. He examined the gold Rolex engraved with our names and the date and admired it, front and back. "Thank you, Marilyn. It's a beautiful memento."

"Yes, I said, a reminder of all the little times we've spent together over the years. It adds up!"

"Unfortunately," he said, "I'll have to squirrel this away for safekeeping until later."

Then we got a knock on the door from security, and I got my good-bye kiss. He said, "You are my *Gloria in excelsis deo*." I didn't need the Latin translation.

May 21, 1962

Dear Red,

I nearly missed our flight yesterday out of Idlewild. Mary Karger came for brunch—Lena prepared bagels and lox and whitefish and egg salad. She said she's worried about me. People dropping dead of overdoses in

Hollywood—the studios have to stop their so-called vitamin shots full of uppers and downers.

"Is Freddy in trouble?" I asked.

"He married Jane Wyman for a second time, and now they're divorced again," Mary replied. Then she got sentimental. "I'm so proud of you, Marilyn, keeping your eye on the ball. You've become a role model for the gals—not just the guys!"

I said, "That's the nicest compliment anyone ever gave me. I know one day it will all go poof, but hopefully my films will last for generations."

Dad explained the "cleanings" immigrant women used to take on the Lower East Side. Abortions really. No one felt a bit of guilt. They understood back then that having another kid or another pregnancy could ruin a family financially. Or kill the mother. Rational decisions were okay back then. Now everything involves a moral twist: divorce, abortion, premarital sex, being a single woman, homosexuality, nudity, even showing an itty-bitty belly button!

MAY 22, 1962

Dear Red,

I have a bad cold, so I practiced my nude swim on paper, like a diagram of a mathematical problem— a splash of my toe here, a backward circular arm movement there, a diagonal twirl across my living room, like a ballerina! Then it's all slapstick climbing out of the pool—one leg over the edge, a little ass, an arched back, the robe slips off my shoulder, a bit of cleavage. Give the camera a little skin at a time and it's not striptease, it's an… accident!

Gee, I never swim in my *own* pool because of the chlorine and what the sun does to my skin.

MAY 23, 1962

Dear Red,

I'm Lady Macbeth, the guilty one with red blood on my hands. It's one of those fucked-up days. Nothing goes right. I'm not bathing or combing my hair or brushing my teeth or exercising. I'm protesting *Marilyn*, staring at this blank page wondering who shines through: Norma Jeane? Zelda Zonk? Is that you-who, Marilyn? I want the gray matter—the brain—not my backside, my smart side.

MAY 24, 1962

Dear Red,

Happy sixty-second birthday, Mother! I'm wearing your silver ring today to remember you. Inez said she gave you my card. I hope you like the roses too. The nurse said you smiled when she told you I'm using the beautiful place mats you wove in your art class. I know you listen. You love Norma Jeane, but you don't dig Marilyn. You're embarrassed that your daughter is a sex symbol, but you like the attention you get being my mother—and you like my fans. Their letters to you are an excuse to preach about Mary Baker Eddy's book *Science and Health*, or Sister Aimee, depending upon the day. If only you took your medication, we could get along.

MAY 25, 1962

Dear Red,

In 1954 Dreamboat was hospitalized with a back injury. I was just back from Canada filming *River of No Return* and a breakup with Joe. I did what every girl can do for a guy in traction: I recited his favorite Keats poem and hung a poster of me on the wall at the end of his bed. We were looking for a private getaway. Helen Hayes had suggested a three hundred–acre French pension with a private landing field upstate New York in a place called Claverack. It means clover field in Dutch. Eleanor Roosevelt had enjoyed the same getaway. I made a call, and they promised a wonderful hairdresser for me. And it worked out! A romantic two-day sail in a cornfield! I remember poetry. Dreamboat said poetry helped him relax. He recited Poe's "The Raven" and the Ancient Mariner and parts of Chaucer. I recited, "There is a certain slant of light," and other short poems—that's the kind I like—Emily Dickenson, Rilke, William Blake, Sappho, Neruda.

I backed Ella Fitzgerald at the Mocambo Club years ago. I sat in the front row every night for a month and we packed the place, broke the color barrier. One night I mentioned to her that I took the train to Hudson. She looked so surprised! She took my hand and told me she was an orphan, like me, and as a teen she was sent to a training school for girls in Hudson. The saddest part was that she wasn't allowed to sing in the choir—it was for white girls only. But she smiled. She said nobody could stop her from singing. When she turned eighteen, she headed straight to Harlem, and launched her career at the Apollo.

May 26, 1962

Dear Red,

Brando came for dinner. We stayed awake almost until dawn holding each other, talking. He is getting married in August, so our time is precious. He said love is heavy, not to be ignored.

"Gee," I said, "for me love is as light as the sunshine. Like a humming bird. Soft clouds. Warm breezes." We laughed. No wonder we're such good friends.

MAY 27, 1962

Dear Red,

Aunt Ida took in boarders. One old man used to give me nickels, and I bought ice cream and candy with these nickels and shared it with the other kids. One day he lured me into his room, held the door shut with his boot, pulled down my panties, and stuck his fingers inside. Aunt Ida warned me to never do that or I would burn in hell. I kicked his leg and ran out. Aunt Ida was at the ironing board. She said to shut up when I told her. I was surprised and confused. I still took his nickels after that, but he never trapped me again.

MAY 28, 1962

Dear Red,

Wow, the nude swim was fun but exhausting! I was in the water for nine hours. I forced everyone off set—only the cameraman and a few photographers I personally invited. I told Paula to go to her hotel too. I laughed, I swam, I splashed, I teased my legs up on the edge of the pool. My back arched in a cat pose. The cameramen went wild clicking. Pat thought it was brilliant. I think the magazines will find it sexy and clean enough to print.

By the way, I'm told my least favorite, Mr. J. Edgar Hoover, keeps a copy of the nude calendar cover of me in his office as a prop so no one will guess he prefers sex with men.

May 29, 1962

Dear Red,

I had a dream that I was traveling in mountains in a strange countryside with people I didn't know. They asked me, "What's wrong? Why are you crying?" I told them, "I have to buy some shoes. I don't have any shoes." Everyone left, but I remained on the mountain. I am alone because I choose to be alone. I'm no longer crying. I say out loud, "Who needs shoes?"

May 30, 1962

Dear Red,

The bitch Dorothy Kilgallen wrote: "If Marilyn could swim, why did she have to pose in the nude?" What is that supposed to mean, anyway? It doesn't make sense. There is no comeback.

Pat says, "Oh, there will be plenty of good hot stuff in the pipeline, Marilyn, don't you worry."

May 31, 1962

Dear Red,

Susie called a day early so she could be the first to sing "Happy Birthday" and tell me she loves me. When I said I'm getting old, she said, "No way, Tinkerbell!" She reminded me of the day Paula brought her backstage to meet me on the set of *Let's Make Love*. Then, when I left Joe, I was suddenly living in her family's New York City apartment! She felt like there were three of us: Susie, Marilyn Monroe, and Anne Frank. A trio of sisters. Anne Frank was born in 1929, only three years after me. It's hard to believe. And all three of us wanted to be film stars! Now look at me. I'm writing a diary!

Here is a little birthday poem I wrote for myself:

I'm singing my nervous curvaceous
"Happy Birthday" song of myself
at thirty-six. My timing is purr-fect.
I'm more than I seem on the big
screen, and still dreaming in color.

I reminded Susie that she dated Richard Burton in those days. She'd come home after a date with Richard, and one night, she was so exhausted, she confused Richard with Peter. "Wait a minute," I interrupted, "did you say Peter and Anne had sex?" We rolled on the floor laughing.

Susie's in love with Christopher Jones now. She's busy—three pictures this year—that makes nine films so far. And she's a guest star on *The Virginian*, a popular cowboy TV show I've heard about. I said I'd take a look at it, but I have a problem with the television commercials—the products people are supposed to buy make me queasy. Uneasy. Cheesy. Creepy. Once I was on the Jack Benny show, and we had some dumb script to read. Then we got squished by an ad for a vacuum cleaner that is supposed to make you feel younger, newer. It seems people can tell any old lie on TV and get away with it.

JUNE 1, 1962

Dear Red,

It's my birthday and the phone is ringing. Andre. Gee, he tried to kiss me last time we bumped into each other—I told him that his photographs of me are some of the best ever, and we should leave it at that. A telegram from Diana Trilling said she was raising her glass to me today! Joe sent roses and his mother's rosary—dark green stone with a large gold crucifix. Maybe I could use it in the night when I can't sleep, the way old Greek men use worry beads. Tonight he's taking me to a muscular dystrophy benefit at Dodger Stadium.

High points of my horoscope: The power to seduce others is as seductive as my own success! I need constant attention. Yes, any of my ex-husbands could tell me that! I learn from my love affairs. Yes. I need to refocus my anger from childhood. No, call it disappointment. I'm just not an angry person. I have vitality, nervous energy and ample hand-eye coordination. True. Optimistic, but unhappy if youthful goals aren't fulfilled. Yep— that's Marilyn.

Pat said she'll drop by the set with a copy of *Time Magazine*: "Marilyn was the hit of the evening." "Now I can retire from politics after having had 'Happy Birthday' sung in such a sweet, wholesome way." Mr. President's words are reprinted everywhere!

JUNE 2, 1962

Dear Red,

Paula hugged and kissed me, a rare show of affection! I completed nineteen shots yesterday, and the rushes look great! A record for me! Birthday cake was served at six o'clock. David Brown gave me a copy of his wife's new book, *Sex and the Single Girl*. She inscribed it, "Dear Marilyn, you are the passionate modern girl. Keep up the good work! Love, Helen." Dreamboat sent a beautiful edition of Keats's collected poems. His note quoted Churchill: "Short words are best, old words are best of all." And the fan clubs sent thousands of birthday wishes.

Now I'm in the early late stage of my life, but I feel like I'm just getting started. I have so far to go. Baby, baby! But baby, it makes me dizzy! I got to hold on to what Dreamboat calls the mischievous, curious kid in me.

That's what he loves. I'm the only women he's ever met with this special thing. He says memories are an important part of life. His brush with death during the war—the loss of siblings Joe and Kick—somehow helps him to live each moment, shrug off his nightmares of enemies chasing him down. Sometimes the enemy wins. I agree. Somebody once said to me the adult world all boils down to shoving off evil or selling beer.

Wouldn't that be something if, one day, women finally gained the right to be independent and grow and change, just like men!

JUNE 3, 1962

Dear Red,

Just finished marking up Skolsky's draft of the Jean Harlow script— it's dramatic and depressing! I guess that's always the case when someone beautiful dies young. She was only in her twenties! It'll be a dream working with Sid. Mother and Aunt Ana were so disappointed when I listened to Arthur and turned down Twentieth Century Fox's production of *The Story of Jean Harlow*. Dad's birthday gift arrived—you guessed it—the biggest bottle of Chanel No. 5 I've ever seen!

Jean Harlow didn't wear underwear. She slept in the nude. She drank champagne. See, what I do is actually nothing new!

JUNE 4, 1962

Dear Red,

Exercised. Nibbled at dark birthday chocolate. Went in disguise to the beach alone. Every transistor radio screamed the hit song: "She-e-e-e-ry! She-e-e-e-ry baby! She-e-rry, can you come out tonight!" At the drugstore on the way home I saw a *Photoplay* headline: America's Two

Queens! Jackie and Liz. Twin brunettes. I guess Pat didn't want to show me that one. When I told her, she said she saw Marilyn Monroe on a short list of film stars Aristotle Onassis made for King Rainier when he was shopping for a glamorous wife. Grace Kelly is the real queen. I would have turned that part down. I only marry for love.

JUNE 5, 1962

Dear Red,

Martin Luther King said somewhere that he got beat up a lot as a kid, and when his father wanted him to fight back, he said, "No. I'm not going to fight them because they aren't thinking when they fight."

Mrs. Murray got on my nerves. Finally, I sent her on errands just to get her out of my hair. I can't stand her being in the house all day. Her habit of sucking air through her teeth, her finger always wrapped in tissue stuck up her nose. Actors know better. But it is really her eyes, her eyes following me, something she tries to conceal. It makes me feel trapped. If I'm living alone, I'd rather be alone.

I turned down a party invitation in honor of Ethel and Bobby. Don't know if Jackie is planning to be there. It's her family. I don't need to fly across the country to attend a party on her turf. It would be asking for trouble. Especially after "Happy Birthday." That created problems for the president. And I promised I wouldn't do that.

JUNE 6, 1962

Dear Red,

I've been *fired*! I called Jack, my lawyer, my agent, my publicist, and Joe. One hundred and four people out of work because of me! Fox is spinning it like I'm loony! All washed up! Just to disgrace me! And replace me! They'll have to learn like the Rat Pack—I'm an institution. I will not fade away. My fans won't stand for it. They are the important people—the leaves of grass! People who keep the planet warm and fed, put gas in cars, flip burgers, dance to Buddy Holly, Billy Holiday, Elvis and Ella, and watch Bette Davis and Bogie and Hitchcock. If Fox ignores the fans, they go out of business.

June 7, 1962

Dear Red,

Inez heard the news. She worries about me. Mother is agitated. I told her I'll find a way out of this mess somehow. Gandhi said a crisis can bring about needed change. So, that's how I'm going to look at this. Dreamboat said, "Babe, they don't know what they're doing." My little old bad news is nothing like the big bad news he has to deal with. Like the little island south of us. He's going to refocus America's imagination and put a man on the moon.

Meanwhile, Cukor called in his thirty-year debt to Hedda Hopper—she got the gossip rags going and announced that my career is over. Joe is ready to go punch Cukor out. That's his answer to everything. Don't know why Cukor turned on me. Rafe is working out the knot on the upper left side of my back.

June 8, 1962

Dear Red,

I'm dodging bullets. Fox has their publicity lined up like a firing squad in *The Hollywood News*. How dare they bad-mouth me when they know they've got *great* footage of *Something's Got to Give*. They *need* me, yet they *dump* me. It's a stunt, to cover up their financial problems. I'm the scapegoat. I sent a telegram to the cast: "Please understand it's not my doing." I need Joe—he's a champ at contracts. Dean Martin called to offer support. "We're going to win this battle," he said. "We're in it together." My fans are lighting up Fox's switchboard like firecrackers.

Bobby called to help. Skouras is in the hospital and can't do anything. Nunnally called him though, and Zanuck, because he believes the footage of *Something's Got to Give* is excellent. Rudin is sticking up for me. He says two films with me will bring in two million. Zanuck is targeting me as insane, linking me with Mother. I *wish* people would shut the fuck up about her.

JUNE 9, 1962

Dear Red,

Fox filed a suit against me for $500,000. Dean too. He will countersue. I was so angry. Pat Lawford begged me to come to dinner. She grabbed my arm as soon as I arrived, and we walked barefoot on the beach into the warm pink sunset. I'm not the only one with problems—it is hard raising four kids. I read Lucille Ball filed for a divorce from Ricky. Divorce is still a bad word in America. I only saw one episode of *I Love Lucy*—Ricky was infatuated with Marilyn Monroe. It was good comedic slapstick.

Norma Jeane. Norma Jeane the human bean. Boring, chlorine, darling, Eileen, Florentine, Georgine, Helene, Imogene, Justine, Maybelline, Opaline … I give up. I bought a new bed and sheets—the finest Egyptian cotton sheets to match the softness of my skin, and a new mattress, and on top of that a European down feather mattress that cradles each arm, each wrist, each finger, leg, and head. Yes, each of my heads.

June 10, 1962

Dear Red,

Dad called to cheer me on. "Kick them in the groin, Marilyn! Give them a black eye! Don't let them get away with calling you meshuggeneh. Pull one of your business stunts. You're smart as a whip, Marilyn, the most powerful woman in the world." I said I plan to turn this problem into a million-dollar contract and get everyone back on the set. "Atta girl," he said. "Go buy yourself a sports car, take a drive into the desert. You'll get through this one, Marilyn. People say you're all woman, but I know you've got a good dose of American testosterone in your blood."

June 11, 1962

Dear Red,

Two hummingbirds at my new feeder! Tashi hung it for my birthday. Speaking of which, the secret vault in the garden is working out well. I told him about the handbag with the false bottom, too. In case anything happens to me, I instructed him to find a publisher. I got a heads up that the White House is launching a new public relations plan to romanticize Jack and Jackie. They are calling it Camelot. I know the limelight is important now, but once he finishes with politics, he'd like a quiet teaching position at a university. We are both on the same page about *how rude* fame really is.

I don't like a man who talks about himself all the time. Dreamboat's mind is open—he listens and *learns*, no matter who he is speaking with. Underneath Jack's presidency, he's sweet. He laughs. He enjoys nature and poetry. My *quirks* don't *irk* him. In fact, they delight him! He loves that I'm not shy about sex. Jackie's father, Black Jack, lost his fortune and needs Dreamboat's money. He figures her spending freedom equals his sexual freedom.

June 12, 1962

Dear Red,

Today is Anne Frank's birthday—she'd be thirty-three! I remember before she went into hiding, her father showed a Rin Tin Tin movie at home for her thirteenth birthday party because Jews were no longer allowed in movie theaters! I met Barras at the beach today for a photo shoot. He lets me take the lead making love to the camera. Like all good photographers, he doesn't fuss when I scratch out the pictures I don't like. The theme today was: *Wake up! I'm alive! Catch me if you can, fox! But you're going to have to pay me what I'm worth!*

June 13, 1962

Dear Red,

I couldn't sleep. At midnight I drove Mrs. Murray's car out into to desert and parked on a dirt road next to an abandoned oil rig that stood like a petrified dinosaur against the sky. I lay on the hood of the car to stargaze. Jimmy and I used to do that a long time ago. The sky pulsed in and out like giant lungs. I have way more physical energy than most people. Working out isn't even enough. I'm still a tomboy—I read that some critic said Jackie is too. Just because she rides horses? Nah, she's ultrafeminine. Artistic. Sophisticated.

I just ran down to the end of the road, touched the oil rig, and ran back to the car. Now I'm out of breath. I jumped back on the hood to wait for the third shooting star. Three is always a lucky number. I'm patient—focused. The planets and stars orbiting in their constellations are a sign that nature is in order. I vow never to lie to my diary. I promise to take myself out more—get out of the Cinderella spin and away from the phone. I can do things like make a salad faster than most people—it's because I have so much I *want* to do. And instead of tiring me, it gives me energy. Except on bad days when I can't get out of bed.

Now I'm rolling my fingers over the sheets, rolling my eyes under the blackout mask, rolling my body side to side. I've taken four Nembutal, two chloral hydrates. I'm skyrocketing right out of Fox's reach. I'm allowed to be late, to stutter when I'm tired, to not finish a sentence, to lie, to muss my hair, to goof lines, to dream in bright colors, to make a living as a sex object, to get paid my fair share, to marry America's best baseball player, America's biggest intellectual, and the president of the United States. To be whatever I want. I can be a single girl who plays hardball like the boys too. I would still play kickball in the street after dinner if somebody knocked on my door and asked me to.

In my dream I was working in the Radio Plane factory inspecting parachutes like I did when I was married to Jimmy. Chico Marx was there, and he kept interrupting my work. Finally, my boss got mad and told him to get his hands off me. I wasn't kissing her, he said. I was whispering in her mouth!

June 14, 1962

Dear Red,

Kind words from *Show Business Illustrated*: "The greatest thing about Marilyn Monroe is not her chest. It's her ear. She is a master of delivery. She can read comedy better than anyone else in the world." And I also read today the opposite: "Marilyn's two best points are between her neck and her waist."

JUNE 15, 1962

Dear Red,

I wish sometimes you could speak to me. I'm extremely fatigued. Tension is a physical strain wrecking my nervous system. It always happens with a film shoot. Mable Todd calls it the explosive overflow of nervous energy. I need to be perfect—not in life, no one can do that, but it *is* possible to be perfect on film. No matter what the director or the producer says, I work for all audiences, including the audience who is not yet born. But the noise from the president's birthday still echoes in my head.

"Pat," I said. "Maybe you should call Sammy Lewis at the New Frontier Hotel and make a megadeal for me, like Frankie and Elvis. I could do a stage show in Vegas. I could pack the house. I love a live audience."

"No way! No, no, no!" She stood up and put her hands on her hips and shook her head. "Every magazine in the world wants an exclusive, Marilyn, and I've begun to say yes. You are booked for the next month. Just because you got fired, you're not over the hill. Not yet. You're a baby at thirty-six. Besides, that venue would kill your film prospects right now."

"Gee, I guess I'm too hurt to see it that way."

"Marilyn," she said, "this kind of drama is nothing more than an opportunity."

JUNE 16, 1962

Dear Red,

I'm trembling with disbelief. Dean Martin stood up like King Kong! He said no to Fox, no to Kim Novak as a costar—nothing personal, but he'll only perform with me. Gee, I'm so grateful. He's my first real big brother sticking his neck out for me. It gives me the opportunity to push through the new contract. I sent a note to all 104 cast members that said things are looking up. I woke at 4:10 a.m. and wrote Dean a thank-you note. I feel my dreaded period coming—I've got cramps.

Thinking so fondly of Dean made me remember my half brother. I never knew him, but I wish I could have. He died a teenager in Tennessee when I was a toddler—another reason for Mother's permanent broken heart. Bernice, my half sister, said he was a nice boy. I didn't meet Bernice until I was working on *Niagara*. We used to write letters, and then we began talking on the phone at holidays, and we even had a family gathering. She visited me in Los Angeles. She is sweet and respects my privacy, but it is not easy to be close. Bernice's husband was starstruck by Arthur when they visited us in New York. Bernice and I gazed into a mirror, matching our ears, our eyes. We had the same thick hair and Mother's thin waist and freckled skin, but that was about it. She has a sweet daughter too.

June 17, 1962

Dear Red,

Do you read me? I read you. I'm a bloody Lady Macbeth today. Kvetch. Bath. Blood. Cramp. Period. Pain. Pills. Dr. G Barks. Bites. Read. Write. Hey. Wake up, Marilyn. I'm reading *Sex and the Single Girl* by Helen Gurley Brown. It's got ammunition. *1) When girls feel sorry for themselves, they get beat. 2) Single women are one of the most maligned minority groups! 3) Being smart about money is sexy! 4) Resist identifying with Mother! 5) There's nothing wrong with being a sex object.* She mentioned me three times in the book. The last mention was in a list of sexy women over the age of thirty-five—wow, she timed that seventeen days close! I guess I shouldn't care.

June 18, 1962

Dear Red,

I found myself humming, "Better watch out, better not shout" this morning. Now what would Anna Freud say about that? A warning to Fox? Singing is a great way to keep vibrant. I would like it, Red, if you could sing along with me. I sing Frankie and Ella tunes while memorizing my lines. Singing makes me feel unlonely when I'm alone, and Frankie and Ella are my two favorites.

I'm scratching the Cinderella story out of the kids' books. Cinderella is weak, and we shouldn't let ourselves fall into that trap. I did the right thing when I bought my own house, especially when it's empty of people. Even waiting for my furniture in an empty house doesn't bother me anymore. Maybe I should tell Mrs. Murray that I'm finished with decorating. I really don't need her services.

Reading back through my diary, I see a pattern of shitty moods and untruths, even though I said I would not lie in these pages. Is not telling the whole truth the same as lying? Not exactly. I just don't put down *all* my struggles. How could I? Paper is like film—it can't capture everything, but it must have enough truth to make it real. When I see my words on paper, I want to dig behind and between them. But that would be clinical practically, like therapy. The truth might be camouflaged on the page right in front of me. So I can return to it and have the chance to recognize it on a second reading.

Give me a glass of Champagne and I'll show you Marilyn Monroe. Say hello to me on a nice day and I'll recite you a line from Shakespeare.

JUNE 19, 1962

Dear Red,

Helen Gurley Brown says to *borrow* kids. Isn't that what I do? I love them all. They help me stay curious and young. Conversations with kids are almost always more interesting than with their parents. Some people think I'd be a flaky mother, but I don't think so. Arthur and I were once contacted by an anonymous woman who wanted us to adopt her baby. Gee, that was sad. We already had a full house with Janey and Bobbybones on the weekends, Sugar Fine the Siamese cat, Ebony the horse, Hugo the basset hound, and Butch and Bob, our parakeets.

Tennessee Williams says: "Make voyages. Attempt them. That's all there is." So true! It's the trip that is of value. Most of what anyone does ends in failure. That's why Red is good for me. Because every day I get another try at using short, old words.

JUNE 20, 1962

Dear Red,

Dr. G is the bully on the playground. He wants to make my friends disappear. The people who love me. The people who support me. When I disagree with him, he calls me hysterical and calls Dr. E to stick me with a needle. I was having lunch at a little place in Venice with Pat when Dr. E showed up. He dragged me into women's bathroom and gave me a shot. Dr. G's orders, he said. Then he started blubbering about his wife divorcing him. I ran out.

When I told Pat what happened, she freaked out. "Your doctor hunted you down, Marilyn! He drugged you!" She lectured me to fight back. She was crying by the time we got to the car.

I tried to calm her down. I said, "It's not that big of a deal, Pat. What bothers me is that doctors have to make sure their patients are sick."

"Your doctors are abusing you," she said.

"I'll drive," I said. I like driving her red Volkswagen bug. I asked her to come in when we got to my house, but she was too upset. She said she'd see me tomorrow.

June 21, 1962

Dear Red,

Sex and the Single Girl: Accept all parts of your body as worthy and loveable, even menstruation as proof of fertility. It isn't easy, but I try. I read when all I can do is bleed. Plato says there's Eros, friendship, and goodwill for all men (he means people). I'm strongest in goodwill. Love has always been more complicated, and friendship is magical. I have my old friends—new friends don't come along very often.

Lee said, "Darling, use the fact that you don't have any women friends—that all women are jealous of you," when I was reading the script for *Some Like It Hot*. That shocked me because I *do* have some long-term loyal women friends. I thought he knew me better. Not all women are jealous.

Rafe came to give me my nightly massage. I told him my fears. He reminded me in one brief sentence and then a peck on the cheek: "Your doctors are living off you, Marilyn. Like parasites." I promised I'd take care of myself.

June 22, 1962

Dear Red,

I made the cover of *LIFE*. My ninth time. "They Fired Marilyn: Her Dip Lives On," it said.

Pat was revived. "Marilyn, you are gorgeous!" she said. "The body does not lie."

I gave Pat a copy of *Sex and the Single Girl*. She's never really opened up about her love life—I wonder why. She's a seriously committed career gal. I should make more of an effort to get to know her personally. She really cares.

Helen Gurley Brown says that way too many women sit life out on the sidelines. Women, Negros, Mexicans—everybody's story needs to be up on the big screen.

June 23, 1962

Dear Red,

Bert Stern is a sweetheart. He brought Dom Perignon and music by the Everly Brothers for the shoot at the Bel Air Hotel on Stone Canyon Road. I stopped for a facial and pedicure at Rebba's Salon and was late, but Bert understands—a girl's got to keep her dignity. The camera and my body are *my* instruments. Macbeth murdered sleep, and Marilyn murdered privacy, someone said. Sometimes good things fall apart so better things can fall together. I like to keep that in mind negotiating with Fox.

June 24, 1962

Dear Red,

Levathes, the new head of Twentieth Century Fox, came over today at my invitation. I wore a turquoise Emilo Pucci shift and served cocktails. I showed him respect, and I demanded it in return. He was shocked at how professionally I manage my image. I had sorted neat piles of over a thousand photographs on the white carpet and asked which image Fox wants to promote. It's really my choice, but I wanted to get to know his take on Marilyn Monroe. It was two hours of powerful work. It felt good! I think I've learned a bit about politics from you know who.

Being first lady was never the right role for me. We decided back in Claverack, Dreamboat, as a former president, will be a free man to do all the things he loves. And I will be the creative director of the Marilyn Monroe Shakespeare Company. We will have dogs, a garden, a small sailboat, and privacy. That is our dream.

June 25, 1962

Dear Red,

I sent Dreamboat a care package of herbs from my garden—lemon verbena and lavender. He likes to soak in a hot bath when he is distressed. In December, he was relaxing with his eyes closed, and he said, "I'm going to send you instructions about bomb shelters."

"What do you mean?" I asked.

"In case of a nuclear attack."

"Is there going to be another war?"

"I'm doing everything I can to prevent it."

I put my finger on his lips and sang a little song. When I stopped, he recited Frost: "The woods are lovely, dark and deep, but I have promises to keep, and miles to go before I sleep."

JUNE 26, 1962

Dear Red,

Whitey fixed my hair hours ago. I just have to do my makeup. I'm two hours late, and here I am writing to you, Red. The way I see it, I'll have less time to deal with the starlets floating through the cocktail hour. Dinner is in honor of the general, so I do want to attend. I wish Dreamboat would make a surprise appearance. He makes me feel like I've just been born. Helen Gurley Brown says, "Work like a beast, cook with seaweed, embrace yoga, know Shakespeare, sandpaper your calloused heels, organize your closets, and read when you are bored." Good advice. I haven't tried the seaweed yet.

Breakfast: black coffee, grapefruit
Lunch: peanut butter and jelly sandwich, black coffee
Dinner: shrimp cocktail, bubbly

JUNE 27, 1962

Dear Red,

Pat and the general had a lively swim in my pool this afternoon. He dove under and around her as she tried to swim laps. Like two kids, they upped each other with cannonballs, jackknives, and backward flips. Later, in the shade, he whispered that at a recent meeting Hoover pushed an envelope across the table containing photographs of Jack's sexual escapades. Then

Bobby pulled out his own envelope and slid it across the table to Hoover. It was a draw.

The general assumes my house, like the Lawfords, is bugged and will only speak out by the pool. "Even the marble bath?" I asked. "Because the tub is the special place a certain person likes to you know what." The general says he's not too worried because as long as both sides have dirt, neither will leak anything to the press. I asked, "Shouldn't the press be covering big important social problems like segregation, education, and poverty?"

June 28, 1962

Dear Red,

Whitey did my makeup for my big meeting with Fox. Agnes did my hair. I rehearsed with Joe. The studio was swamped with journalists. Fox tried to strip me of my contract, but Frosch argued for a two-film million-dollar deal. To get this, I'll have to make concessions: 1. Accept a new director. Okay, sorry, Cukor. 2. Get rid of Paula! Oh, my God! How will I tell her? 3. The big bomb: Frosch, my attorney, told me to *read every word* of the last contract. Three times Rudin tried interrupt me. Well! Fox paid Dr. G $10,000 to make sure I got to work on time. That's on top of what I pay him. He's no doctor. He's a sneaky fucking imposter thief.

My head hurts. I agree to get rid of Paula. I've got to think this through. Who to trust? Dr. G is so fucked up because he made sure I need him. He thinks he controls me, but I've already proven that wrong.

Shit List

Dr. G
Rudin
Mrs. Murray
Weinstein

Trusted Friends

Frosch
Pat
Lee
Rafe
Dr. E
Inez
Pat Lawford
Whitey and Marjorie
Joe
Anne and Mary Karger

JUNE 29, 1962

Dear Red,

I met Paula at her hotel this morning after I worked out so I could break the news to her myself, before she reads it in the Hollywood papers. I gently explained that to get a new contract, I have to make concessions, and she is one of them.

"I brought you this gift in appreciation for all you've done for me," I said, and clasped my pearls around her neck. "These were given to me by the Japanese emperor on my honeymoon with Joe."

She finally looked up: "It's bashert. But Lee will be furious, Marilyn. You are his most famous student, and you are turning your back on us."

"I'll call him," I said.

Lee didn't pick up the phone—it was the housekeeper, someone I didn't recognize. He hasn't called back. Not good, because certainly by now Paula has reached him. Surely he won't blame Paula. Unfortunately, Paula gets the short end of the stick. Susie told me that once she went to a party in New York and saw her father on the couch across from her kissing a young starlet. He never spoke to Susie about it. She said after that she had to get out of New York, out from under his spell.

Dreamboat's private number has been blocked—I can't get through! I always got through before. Agnes fixed my hair for the *Cosmo* shoot with George Barris. Anita Loos's representative called to see if I was interested in a new musical based on blah blah blah. Please call my agent, I said. I'm too upset to think about anything else! I need to relax. I called Rafe for a massage.

"Imagination and water are wedded forever," Dreamboat read from Moby Dick at the French pension in Claverack when I turned my nose up at the book. But that line got me hooked: imagining while reading is what makes books so profound. I've been forced to deal with plenty of great whites. The world is full of them. Imagination is the key to survival.

JUNE 30, 1962

Dear Red,

Agnes, my hair angel, came to my house again. She brought me coffee, dressed me, fixed my hair, straightened my room. Every day is new, Marilyn, she said. There are good doctors and bad doctors. Get rid of Dr. G. Take a look at what he's been pumping you with. Ouch. That sounds bad. It was the second photo shoot for *Cosmo*, and it went swell. But now I'm awake. Too much to think about. Lee is sore and hasn't returned my call. I took two more pills. If only I could say good night to Dreamboat every night like I used to.

Bobby stopped by as Jack can't. Too much political pressure. I get that. Touching Bobby is like touching Jack. He is kind, funny, smart, and fascinating to listen to, but his pursuit of the Mafia scares me. Both brothers are excellent at driving home their point. He brought up my diary before he left. "Burn it," he said.

I called Dr. G tonight and dropped the bomb—that I found out about his $10,000 agreement with Fox. Five minutes later, he showed up at my house.

I said, "Stop sending Dr. E to chase me down. It's humiliating."

Dr. G said, "I'm doing what needs to be done, Marilyn."

"Go to hell," I said, and pushed him out the door. In the morning I'll call A-1 locksmith about getting the locks changed.

JULY 1, 1962

Dear Red,

I'm exhausted. Pat said I looked like shit when she arrived. How could I look like anything but shit? I didn't get any sleep last night. It took me hours to get into Marilyn this morning. Agnes came at one o'clock and did my hair for the third and last *Cosmo* shoot. I asked Mrs. Murray to leave. After that I felt more comfortable. I put on casual cantaloupe-colored slacks and a matching top and worked with Meryman for five and a half hours. "Please don't make me look like a joke," I said as he was leaving.

Pat said that I was a little on the edge. Maybe I shouldn't have said that to Richard Meryman. Readers don't want to know that I care about Negros and Mexican workers, and the poor single mothers trying to feed their kids, or that Tashi was forced to change his name to Tommy when he and his parents were sent into a camp from their island in Puget Sound during the war because they are Japanese. That's not sexy. Not the news they want. There's only one side of me the media is interested in. It reads like this: thirty-six, twenty-four, thirty-six. And this: she's an orphan.

She pops pills. She's divorced three times, poor thing. And poor thing, no children. And poor thing, her mother is crazy.

July 2, 1962

Dear Red,

Inez stopped by to sign Mother's papers, write checks, and take care of some of her mail. Her doctors are not labeling her a schizophrenic anymore. Instead, she has agoraphobia and paranoia—not bipolar like the newspapers used to say. Inez and I agree that Mother simply gave up on the world. This is why she refuses medication! In reality she's fit. She's going to live a long life. Maybe I'd better increase her trust fund.

Dreamboat and I have the same pain *and* fame, only he has a beautiful wife the world loves. I have the camera, the telephone, Maf, and Red. I don't have to bitch or get hysterical to get the attention I need. Red is at my side. And I don't have to comb my hair or get out of bed. Red doesn't judge and never thinks I'm crazy when I don't put on makeup, or when I walk around the house naked. I am whoever we want to be, any day of the week. Writing in Red makes me free.

I was photographed today in the bow pose—it's Kundalini yoga. On my belly, arms over my head, I grab my feet and rock on my belly button!

July 3, 1962

Dear Red,

I can't get through to Jack or the general. Yeah, yeah, yeah, I know the story: politics. Big problems are brewing. "Keep calm and carry on," he reminds me. Finger off the dial. It's politics. Have to say good-bye for now. Break the habit. Actors know how to do that. He couldn't marry me because I was divorced, and I wasn't catholic. But he recently confessed a secret first marriage that was annulled. When his brother Joe was killed in the war, his father turned to him to fulfill the family dream of gaining the White House. One day he'll be ready to take on the eighth wonder of the world. *Me!* He likes my approach to his problems, that I can warm up the cold images of his mother who was never around for him. He said the biggest thing she ever did for him was serve hot tea for American ladies when he campaigned.

July 4, 1962

Dear Red,

I left a message at Hyannis Port for Jack. I know I'm not supposed to call. I just want to wish him a happy July Fourth. That's not really calling, is it? I gave Mrs. Murray the day off—and I'm hosting a party. Inez is helping. Tashi, his wife and daughter, Rafe, Whitey and Marjorie, Agnes and her kids, Pat, Joe, and a few others. I've ordered from Briggs Deli, but I'm making my favorite recipes, too: potato salad with caviar, oysters on the half shell, homemade noodle salad with fresh basil, Joe's mother's recipe, and fruit balls, and grilled salmon steaks marinated in sake.

Jack told me if you want peace, prepare for war. What we share is in saecula saeculorum. I learned my tactics from him, so when the general returned my call and ordered me to lay off Jack, I gave him hell.

July 5, 1962

Dear Red,

Maybe talent all boils down to how well you can observe. It's tough training to be nonjudgmental because you can't really learn if you are busy deciding if something is morally right or wrong. Andy sent me a birthday gift. A beautiful self-portrait drawing on three pieces of paper, a triptych—very light and delicate. Warhol is in the center of a flower garden, nude, smiling—a full frontal view, with both male and female genitals. Very clever. A new species for Darwin to study. It's hanging in dining room, if the table ever arrives from Mexico.

July 6, 1962

Dear Red,

Agnes had to fix my hair again. She says she doesn't mind. She needs the work now that *Something's Got to Give* is canceled. I told her not to worry—it'll get rolling again soon. I had a *Life* interview. Pat had requested the questions in advance so I had time to work my answers. She said I was in perfect form—funny, deep, articulate!

Pat, Rafe, and Joe have the new keys. Everyone else has to knock, including Mrs. Murray and Dr. G.

July 7, 1962

Dear Red,

I'm stuck in my room. Something fucked happened. It is difficult to write because Dr. G is standing guard. He took my phone away and barricaded my bedroom door to the pool. I'm a caged tiger. I can barely lift my head, but my tail is whipping around. Claws and teeth are visible. It started on the phone, and then Dr. G was banging at my door. I said I was going to call the cops, and he quieted down. He begged me to open up, and I mistakenly did. He was shaking and disheveled. I said it looked like he just crawled out from beneath the couch. He smacked me across the cheek. Then he hit me across my nose. I landed on the floor, bleeding.

"*Don't touch me,*" I said when he tried to apologize. I made him drive me to my surgeon.

When Joe and I were married, Joe used to yell at me to tell me shut up. He didn't have any other words. He's old school. He thinks women shouldn't have an opinion, that women should obey him. Yelling at me is like taking a dump—it makes him feel better. After he yells, he's calm. I used to say, "Wait, you are out of control. Let me turn on the tape recorder so I can show you what you sound like." I'd laugh and he'd get angry. After the press shoot for *Seven Year Itch*, I drove to Nevada and got a divorce.

July 8, 1962

Dear Red,

Dr. G apologized a dozen times. He said he was jealous, stupid, emotional, paranoid. He covered the mirrors so I can't see myself. He took my phone and locked the doors. But I can feel how bad I look. Luckily nothing is broken. I'll be okay. I have to rest. Drink lots of hot tea. Wear plenty of makeup when I go out next week. In the meantime, Dr. G is babysitting me. He told the surgeon I fell in the shower, like I was drunk!

Joe's excuse way back when was that he was the jealous type. Italian, just like his father. "No, you're the physically abusive type," I said. The act of contrition doesn't work in my book. Tonight I'm angry at Joe all over again. I wish I could just drive to Nevada and divorce Dr. G.

Dr. E was just here to give me a "vitamin" shot. Dr. G told him I fell in the shower. Why did I keep my mouth shut and let him lie? The right half of me is sweating and the left half cold and shivery.

Dr. G was asleep on the couch, so I tried calling Jack. I took my phone back into my room. I tell Jack everything. I forgot RE7-8200 no longer accepts my calls. When I asked Jackie about the birthday gift *she* got from Joe Sr., she laughed: why only one million when I could have asked for ten?

JULY 9, 1962

Dear Red,

"What are you staring at?" I said to Mrs. Murray this morning when Dr. G finally left. I soaked in Chanel No. 5, washed my hair, looked at my black and blue eye and swollen nose, and for the first time, I cried. I'm going to get dressed, put on makeup, and take Maf on a walk, right past Mrs. Murray, to the phone booth where I can finally get some privacy. I need to take back my life. On my way out, I paused in front of Lincoln's portrait—think of what he suffered when his beloved son died!

JULY 10, 1962

Dear Red,

Yoo-hoo. Marilyn? Any little old me at home today? I'm trying to seduce myself. I want an intimate date with me. I want to dream hard and feel what I feel in my own backyard. I want to take care of myself. Pat Lawford called her brother from a girlfriend's house, then handed me the phone. Jack was at Hyannis Port, visiting his ill father. He said, "Russia is building a naval shipyard disguised as a fishing village. Do you understand what this means, Marilyn? We have a crisis building. I'm working on a plan, so Russia can save face. He said, "I love you." I smiled and said it back to him.

July 11, 1962

Dear Red,

Agnes fixed my hair for the Fox meeting today. She saw my bruise beneath the makeup. She of course doesn't ask for an explanation. She listens and guesses and talks around subjects so I can bare my soul. I told her I fired Paula to make way for the new contract. She knows it is a very personal decision and applauded me and told me how hard it must be. Fox was expecting a scene—but I made it just plain business.

July 12, 1962

Dear Red,

Another meeting with Fox. I chose Jean Negulesco as director to finish *Something's Got to Give.* Twentieth Century Fox has agreed to go back to Nunnally's script—a much funnier, sexier version than what it mushed into. We are closing in on the kill ... and luckily, no animal will be harmed. It'll be a win-win for both sides.

Gee, my accountant said someone is skimming money off the books, hundred thousand so far. "It couldn't be Inez or Hedda, who reads my fan mail," I said. "I trust them."

"Marjorie Stengel?" he asked.

"No," I said, "she never had access."

"Maybe one of your attorneys?"

When I hung up, I wondered if it was *him.* My accountant. A friend of you know who— Weinstein, Dr. G, Mrs. Murray, and Frosch! I'll have Joe's attorney look into it.

JULY 13, 1962

Dear Red,

My nose is finally looking its unfruity self. Dr. G is feeling vulnerable. He is afraid I'm writing about *it* and *him*. I told him I burned my diary at the general's insistence. I've come up with a plan—I told Dr. G that I'll make a tape recording for him. I'll be very busy so he'll have to stay away. He thinks it will be a valuable piece of me, something he can share with Anna Freud, but in reality, it will be the same old crap—nothing new. I can record it in the middle of the night when I can't sleep.

Meanwhile, I'm making some major personnel changes. I've ordered a locked gate for my driveway.

JULY 14, 1962

Dear Red,

I threw a twentieth birthday party for Joan, Dr. G's daughter. She invited two dozen friends, her parents, and their friends, and we all hung out around the pool. The girls looked beautiful in their bikinis. Joe sat by my side all afternoon while Dr. G and his wife sunbathed. Finally, we had cake—it's a Julia Child's recipe, with two pounds of butter and a dozen eggs, an apricot center, and coconut whipped cream frosting. I gave Joan the mink stole I wore to the Golden Globe Awards ceremony. Her mother wasn't happy. My real birthday present to her is teaching her how to do a striptease, but that we did in private yesterday.

JULY 15, 1962

Dear Red,

Mrs. Murray broke my weight-lifting routine when she arrived at eight this morning. I jumped up and insisted that she take the day off—she had put in extra hours for the party. I literally had to shove her out the door. All I wanted was to enjoy my empty house and heal my face. And if I want to write in Red, I don't have to hide. If I want to dance naked or have sex with a delivery boy on the living room floor, she won't be there to report it to Dr. G.

I'm going to give Florence Thomas a call, see if she wants to be my housekeeper again. She kept my place spic and span. Dr. G talked me into getting rid of her when I bought my house. I messed up.

JULY 16, 1962

Dear Red,

I told Agnes that I have an appointment in two weeks with Dr. A. I'm taking her advice and dumping Dr. G. She lectured me about hanging out with the Rat Pack when I told her that it was Pat and Peter Lawford taking me to Cal Neva. Hopefully Frosch and Rudin will finish up negotiations on the contract by next week. Agnes seemed relieved. She kissed both cheeks and said, "Take care of yourself, sweetheart."

JULY 17, 1962

Dear Red,

Blood smeared my sheets like a rusty sunset with the pain of yet another period. Every time I complain, my GYN doctor offers to do a hysterectomy. There are now replacement hormones, but I think natural is best. I'm afraid of menopause, and droopy breasts, and depression setting in. Best let the blood run. At least my face is healing. But eight days later, I still have to wear an extra layer of foundation to cover the bruise. It's turned yellow.

JULY 18, 1962

Dear Red,

When I was a kid, a dog named Tippy followed me around—the cutest, most loyal mutt you ever saw. He followed me to school, and at lunch I fed him my peanut butter sandwich, and after school he was still there waiting for me. Aunt Ida let me keep him, so I bathed him and cleaned up after him, and he slept in my bed. But one day he disappeared. We finally found him shot dead in a neighbor's garden. We dug a grave in the backyard, but nothing could stop me from crying. Aunt Ida was afraid I'd starve to death, so she had Mother come and get me.

Mother and I set up a house after that just down the street from Aunt Ana, so I could go there after school. Mother liked to sing and play the piano, but our little home only lasted about a year. She couldn't handle me, work, and her boyfriends.

I was lying on my back today in my garden, writing, when a little cloud floated by. I smiled. LA doesn't usually have any puffy white friends drop by.

JULY 19, 1962

Dear Red,

Pat and Peter are picking me up tomorrow morning. We are driving to Cal Neva, just over the California border. They say I need a rest, and this is the perfect opportunity. Frankie is scheduled to perform Friday and Saturday nights. I can always relax to his singing.

Right now, I'm out by the pool with Red, and I turned on the transistor radio. Ray Charles is singing, "I can't stop loving you"—and it's true!

July 20, 1962

Dear Red,

Dreamboat sent me a love note, and at the end, he quoted one of the Greeks: "The friend is another self." I'll have to look up that translation.

A new magazine, *Playboy*, bought Lawrence Schiller's photographs of my nude swim scene for $25,000. "Good for him," I said. Joe didn't think so. I need to split the rights to my image. Whatever, I look forward to seeing the photographs published!

July 21, 1962

Dear Red,

The day started nice and cool, drinking coffee by the pool. Out walked Rudin in his swim trunks. I thought I was going to die! I gave him the cold shoulder. He swam a few laps and left me alone. I started pacing like a trapped animal. Then I spotted Joe standing on the hill outside of the compound. I waved. Joe wasn't welcome at Cal Neva. He and Frankie had a falling out a long time ago. Joe hates when I hang out with the Rat Pack. But Frankie has been part of my life since I was sixteen. And Pat and Peter are some of my best friends. Joe is jealous.

JULY 22, 1962

Dear Red,

Bad, bad, bad, bad. Last night was fucked up. Frankie was singing on stage. Giancana sat down next to me at a front row table. About fifteen minutes later, he pushed another highball at me, and I watched as he put two fingers in his mouth, slobbering all over them, wondering what the hell. Next he had my head in a lock hold, my face smashed to his chest, and he poked his finger up my ass, making the whole thing look like a big hug. We had a scuffle, and I broke out of his clutch. I said in a low voice, "I'm not your goddamn table ornament," and tossed my drink in his face. Frankie caught sight of it from stage and nearly stopped singing. I ran out of there stuttering and tripped and fell on my knees, hyperventilating. I couldn't get any words out. Flashes went off, and I realized Giancana's goons photographed the whole fucking setup.

Later Frankie visited my cottage and tried to soothe me. "Just apologize to Giancana," he said.

"What for, like I disrespected him?" I yelled.

"Everyone knows you don't wear underwear, and he said he always wanted to see if he could pull it off."

"Fuck you, Frankie. You were in on it! Whose friend are you, anyway?"

"I'm trying to help," he said. "Everyone but you know, knows your 'lover' Bobby is in Los Angeles this weekend. That's why the Lawfords got you out of the way."

"Bobby is *not* my lover, you idiot!" I screamed. I started throwing things at him to get him to leave.

"Okay, okay, I should keep my big trap shut," he said, and he poured me a bourbon and pushed sleeping pills into my mouth. "Here's to the confusion of our enemies."

I think I'm finally over Frankie. It's been twenty years. He tried this shit once before with his buddies, breaking into an apartment to catch me sleeping with a woman. *But they got the wrong apartment,* and the woman there pressed charges against them for breaking and entering. They had to pay the woman off. The real punch here is Pat and Peter, fooling me into coming to a quiet weekend at Cal Neva. Why? Who was giving them orders? Joseph P. Kennedy? Hoover? Bobby? Jack? FBI? CIA?

I locked myself in my cottage and wouldn't open up for Pat. I let her cry and bang on the door. I swallowed two more sleeping pills and a chloral hydrate and sobbed into my pillow until I fell asleep. I want off the merry-go-round. I want only loyal friends. I am sick of being toyed with by the Kennedys. By the Mafia. Being stalked by Joe. Fighting Fox. Pat said she let herself in later with a key when the switchboard found my phone off the hook. She kissed and rocked me like a baby and apologized and said she loved me and poured black coffee down my throat. I heard her tell Peter I was in a barbiturate haze. She got me dressed, telling me Bobby didn't have time to see me. She swore she was done with "family" orders. At dawn, Frank's pilot flew the three of us back to LA.

July 23, 1962

Dear Red,

Mrs. Murray was standing in the driveway with Weinstein having a private conversation when I woke up. What is she thinking? Is she describing my "delicate" condition to him? She didn't know I saw her, but as soon as she walked in, I gave her notice and handed her six months of severance pay. She took it like ice, but agreed to stay on until the fourth, and Florence starts on the fifth. I finally did something that makes me feel empowered. It's the right thing. I called Rafe, and he congratulated me. He came over and gave me a double-long massage, his strong hands easing the bad karma out of my every little muscle, while I mumbled my stream of problems.

Dr. G said I was making a mistake firing Mrs. Murray, and he reminded me that I made the mistake before and I regretted it. "Remember when you had no one to drive you on errands when you didn't feel up to it?" he said.

"I am capable of hiring a car," I told him. "Besides, I don't like her."

I had to stop myself. I almost blurted too much. I chewed the right side of my cheek until I tasted blood. They are friends or business partners. Yes. I will get rid of him too, but right now I need to remain calm. When I think about getting rid of him, my head jams up, because he is going to fight it. He's got my whole life rigged, and I'm chicken to cut off his head. It's like cutting my own damn neck. He knows and I know. It's a bad dance. We're stepping all over each other.

JULY 24, 1962

Dear Red,

I took Maf for a jog around the Brentwood loop before anyone woke up. We listened to the birds, smelled fragrant lemons in the early heat. I may sell this house when I settle in New York. I love my garden and privacy when I get it, but the rest is a disappointment. I finally had a conversation with Lee. He has me focused. He's looking forward to seeing me in a few weeks. I told him about Dr. G's abuse. For right now, he wants me to concentrate on the exercises.

July 25, 1962

Dear Red,

Instead of sleeping, I remembered years ago that Betty Grable told me about fame. She said, "Honey, I've had it. Go get yours. It's your turn now."

Then a film I saw popped into my head called *The Other America*. And I thought, instead of practically bleeding to death every month, I could have a hysterectomy. I could adopt a couple of kids. I know there is probably a requirement for adoption, like two parents, but I see single divorced women raising great kids all the time. And the truth is, there are plenty of kids who don't have either parent!

July 26, 1962

Dear Red,

I made up with Pat Lawford. I know getting me out of town wasn't her idea. Pat promised never to deceive me again. I went to dinner at their house. The general was there. We walked out onto the beach, and he told me that Hoover has a report on me: "Security Matter 105–C." C is for communist. It's a foreign intelligence matter. Hoover told the general that I blabbed to my friends about the first known detonation of the H-bomb on US territory. This is the reason Jack has had to sever ties. *Sever ties* with me! I crumpled to the ground and cried, and he kissed me and stood me back up on my feet and said, "We are all in this together." It's not so bad. Jack shouldn't be telling me such things. We're all under surveillance. We can't be too careful. And right now none of us should be taking unnecessary risks. I spelled L-O-V-E in the sand and hit my chest. Bobby grabbed me, stroked me, cooed to me.

"Then you won't risk his presidency or his life," he said.

"You want me to shrivel up like a dried flower?"

"No, since you know true love, you know it's perennial. Another time and place, your love can flourish. Promise you won't call?"

"I will never do anything to hurt Jack," I promised.

I'm in bed writing. Peter isn't strong. He has no courage or personal conviction. He does what he is told and is too dependent on others. This is what Pat's been trying to tell me. Of course, she can't really say it. She's not ready to make her move. She's got the kids to think about, but she detests being part of their schemes while Peter is happily sucked in.

JULY 27, 1962

Dear Red,

I tried calling the general to talk more about the report. I didn't ask many questions. I was so worried about Jack and me. Now I'm worried about what I blabbed, who I blabbed to, and where I was and when I took those drugs he says I took. Because I don't remember talking about the H-bomb. We did talk about the history of Cuba, or I should say, I listened. I heard all about the handsome Che Guevara—no matter what side of politics you are on, his dedication to justice is impressive—and thanks to the president, the US Special Forces now have permission to wear green berets.

I wonder if anyone has secretly read my diary. The photographs they claim they have must be much more damaging. It was an awkward conversation with the general, and he really was kind about it. Does J. Edgar Hoover *really* have something on tape? I think he is *making it up*, just to shut me up. Bobby is yet another mouthpiece, doing his job. He doesn't know if it's true.

July 28, 1962

Dear Red,

Pat said I'm on the cover of *Life* next week. We went through our calendar: I've got *The Jean Harlow Story* with Sidney coming up. Ms. Caswell, he calls me, the girl with the horizontal walk. He was my best publicist back in my early days. He kept my name in the papers and helped profile Norma Jeane. I've got a Frosch appointment to change my will on Monday and a press conference. And Lee Thompson, to talk about *What a Way to Go* with costar Gene Kelly. And a hair appointment with Battelle. On September 27, I have a date with Dreamboat in DC. And of course, I want to have dinner with the Rostens in Brooklyn Heights. I'm putting my poems together for him, more than thirty he can select from for a book. And I have a meeting with Jule Styne about *A Tree Grows in Brooklyn*. Frankie is costarring in that. Yes, we've made up. He acknowledged that his "friends" were in the wrong.

Love is complicated.
Layers of sweet batter,
like a wedding cake—freckled
beneath the frosting:
small, memorable bites.

July 29, 1962

Dear Red,

When I asked Jackie about Camelot, she ignored my questions and said her fantasy is to live in New York and become a writer. She wasn't sure what kind of writer, except nonfiction. And not autobiographical. She has had enough of the limelight. She said, "Marilyn, I'm not brave like you." When she happened to have mentioned Henry Rosenfeld, a mutual friend, a light bulb went off in my head: he may be the perfect business partner for my Marilyn Monroe Shakespeare Company—a wealthy dress manufacturer, a kind and loyal friend. I'll give him a call and try to see him when I'm in New York next week.

PS: My dining room table arrived from Mexico today! Tashi helped me set it up. It's big, heavy, and beautiful, just like I wanted. I am so happy. Warhol's clever self-portrait floats above it. I immediately brought over my one chair, brought out some cold herring and crackers, popped open some bubbly, and sat down to my very own one-person party!

July 30, 1962

Dear Red,

In truth, I feel bad for Paula. But we are both worn out, broken by *Something's Got to Give*. Luckily, Lee won't ever know I'm removing him from my will on Monday—because he doesn't know he is specified to receive the bulk of my assets. I'll work with him in New York, but his anger over the loss of Paula's income hurts me. Paula is always his messenger. She said they are financially dependent on me. But firing Paula is not a reflection on Lee or the method. That part is not personal. I do want to continue working with Lee on my own terms. I'm taking back my life, one step at a time.

July 31, 1962

Dear Red,

I gave Dr. G the tapes—five hours' worth, including lots of pauses and deep breathing. It took many takes to record it light, carefree, without expressing the anger I feel toward him—ringleader of the gang! The tapes do not include anything new, sexy, or controversial. It's icing. But I hope he is satisfied. Keeping him out of my hair will help me separate. Will he publicize them? I don't care. Right now he feels like he struck gold. He has a piece of Marilyn's flesh. Time will reveal who is foolhardy. I already know it is him.

When I think of working with Dean again, I'm not anxious or nervous. His love is something I will always be grateful for. What he did in turning down working with all other actresses was to give me *respect*. And the press shouted it to the world!

AUGUST 1, 1962

Dear Red,

Hallelujah! Amen! At four o'clock this afternoon, I signed a million-dollar two-picture contract with Twentieth Century-Fox and Marilyn Monroe Productions—*Something's Got to Give* along with *What a Way to Go*. I'll be free of Fox in spring of 1963. Zanuck, Weinstein, Frosch, Rubin, Chasin, Levethes, me, Pat, and a dozen others lit up cigars and toasted! I can hardly believe the old contract was a hundred thousand for one film, like I'm a two-bit character actor.

I called Dad to report the swell news. "You did it! Baby, baby, you broke the studio system!" he yelled into the phone. I laughed to think of the wiretap recording the good news. It should reach DC within the hour.

Truman Capote has a *big ear* on the pulse of Hollywood. He called to say he heard the news through the grapevine. He said my power comes to me both ways: sometimes zooming in from outer space, sometimes through grass roots, organically from the ground up. He wants to celebrate next week when I'm in New York.

I called Rafe to ask him to dinner Saturday: champagne and dancing at my house. I'm finally going to teach him the twist.

Eveline Snively called to congratulate me—said she heard from Weinstein. She said, "Marilyn, you are the smartest actress I know. Don't you ever let anyone tell you anything different. There is so much nonsense in Hollywood." I told her I'm proud of myself, too. "Give yourself a pat on the back," she said. "I'm going to give you a big kiss you when I see you."

I got two marriage proposals today. Joe called to say he quit his job; he wants to devote himself to me. We could live anywhere I want in the world.

"Joe," I said. "We tried, remember? I'm a working girl. Don't quit your job for me."

My second proposal came from a sweet billy-goat-looking man who owns a collector's shop on Santa Monica Boulevard, where I bought a coffee table today. He saw my name on the check and asked me to marry him. He couldn't believe it was really Marilyn Monroe. I said, "I can't believe it either."

Then this fucking strange perfumed letter from Jean Smith—Dreamboat's sister I've never met— arrived in the mail. Someone is really fanning the flames. Yes, I like Bobby because he's Jack's brother. Bobby knows the scoop. Maybe he is the one with the fib. She insinuates I'm an item with Bobby! What kind of trick is that! I never was his item! Never will be! I immediately picked up the phone to call the general to find out what this bullshit game is about. No answer. I thought he was close with his sisters. Why is he pulling the wool over their eyes? What the hell is going on!

Thursday, August 2, 1962

Dear Red,

I mistakenly asked Mrs. Murray to drive me to the pharmacy to pick up Dr. E's prescription, which opened me up for an attack. "You should call Dr. G when you need help, Marilyn."

"It's none of your business," I said.

"Marilyn, you misunderstand me," she said.

I ordered her to stop and let me out of the car and told her to be packed and gone by the time I got home.

It was about ninety degrees outside. I was hysterical. I called Dr. E from a phone booth and asked him if he could pick me up. As soon as I was in his car, I vomited all over myself. He kept asking what was wrong. I asked who was he loyal to, me or Dr. G. He swore I was his patient, that he would never betray my confidentiality. So after we cleaned me and the car at his office, I told him about Dr. G's contract with Fox for a sum of $10,000, to get me to the set on time. Dr. E was shocked. I told him about my fight with Mrs. Murray—that she, Dr. G, and Rudin were all ganging up on me. I also told him Dr. G beat me up that weekend he said I had fallen in the shower. He asked why I didn't go to the police, and I told him that Dr. G held me hostage in my house until Monday, when Mrs. Murray arrived. I don't know if Dr. E believed me. He brought me home and gave me a shot to relax, and I told him I was getting rid of Dr. G. He could either team up with my new psychiatrist or quit too. I told him my house is bugged, so everything that happens inside is recorded.

Later, I called Whitey and Marjorie, and they came over to celebrate my new contract. They were very sweet, bringing Champagne and a bucket of caviar. We all toasted to the new beginning. And they witnessed me dumping pills down the toilet. They also suggested I call Pat and ask her to stay with me for a few days. Whitey, like many of my friends, was relieved I was getting rid of Mrs. Murray. He always thought of her as a spy.

Pat said the press is crawling around my neighborhood, even scratching at *her* apartment door! She cancelled the *Playboy* spread. "It's the wrong timing," she said. I was a little disappointed, but she assured me it'll have its day. Thirty magazines are planning to print the nude swim photos! In the meantime, she set up a press conference for Monday afternoon, before my four o'clock appointment with Rudin to change my will. She brought sweet telegrams from everyone in the cast about how proud they are of me for saving the film, and a ton of fan club mail. Joe heard the news before I got a chance to call him and called to congratulate me.

I tried the general again. I'm keeping my promise not to call Jack—but I still want an explanation about Jean's letter.

August 3, 1962

Dear Red,

Pat has bronchitis and stayed over. I'm upset because it's nearly noon and she's still sleeping like a baby. I've been making my phone calls, doing my exercise routine—pushups, weights, and hula hoop. It gives me energy, even when I'm tired. Maf keeps me in shape, too, wanting to play ball all the time. He seems to know your garden vault, Red. He's always scratching and peeing on it. It's waterproof, but still, of all the unsweet things a pooch could do!

Pat called her office and had the mail sent over. I knocked the socks off Liz! Right on the cover of *Life Magazine*—"Marilyn Lets Her Hair Down about Being Famous," a beautiful article! The best ever written about me, though, so much of what I said was left out. This is always the case. Even the ending I was so worried about was fine. I don't mind saying it—I'm *proud* of myself. I called Richard Meryman and thanked him for the sympathetic article. I feel good, like a normal human being!

Next, I read the Dorothy Kilgallen article—"Marilyn's new infatuation is a handsome gentleman who is a bigger name than Joe DiMaggio." Fuck her. She's picking up on that Bobby rumor? I showed Pat Jean Kennedy's letter, but she waved it off, insisting that I not worry about it. Someone just got their gossip crossed.

Pat is brown as a Mexican, smoking Pall Malls in the sun at the pool while I'm the albino in the shade—and she complained of a sore throat! We flipped through her stack of mail and magazines. All afternoon, Carl Sandburg's chimes made music in the breeze—a housewarming gift. I have to send him a letter about what a comfort that sound is to me. And there is a repetitive *ping, ping, ping* from the installation of my new gate at the driveway. Wrought iron, with an electronic control to open it from inside the house—that will help to keep certain persons out. Pat was relieved! I told her I gave Dr. G the tapes I'd been working on as a going-away gift of sorts, and not to worry. There is nothing new in them, but Dr. G feels like he's got something of value. I'm really just placating him; women have to do that sometimes for a peaceful exit.

I told her a little about my lost weekend, asking her just to listen and not say anything, and how Dr. G was paid by Fox to get me to the set on time! Fox gave him that power because they didn't trust *me*. Or he talked them into believing I was his sicko patient. Well, they discovered their error, and the film ground to a halt. Now, after cleaning house, we are starting again. In a few days I'll be done with Dr. G and his gang—his brother-in-law Rudin, Mrs. Murray, Weinstein. And Bernstein! It was also Dr. G who talked Fox into dumping Nunnally and into hiring his friend Walter Bernstein.

Pat and I napped in the shade. She held my hand. She was so upset. She didn't see how I could make it through all the tension. I told her Joe knows the situation and has helped arrange the letters of discharge through my other attorney, Frosch. Joe is my pillar of strength—which she finds weird because Joe took his turn hitting me too. I said, "I think he learned his lesson. Besides, I'm not his wife." She asked me to stay with her for a few days. I thought that was very sweet. I said I might take her up on it.

We had dinner with Peter at La Scala. Pat Lawford was out of town, and Bobby was supposed to show up, but at the last minute told Peter that he couldn't make it. He was in San Francisco with his family. Pat went straight to bed when we got home as she could hardly talk and felt miserable.

It's eleven o'clock. I just had four very disturbing calls. Each was the same female voice. She said, "Marilyn, cut the affair with Bobby."

"Who are you?" I asked. Another time: "I'm *not* having—" but I got cut off.

Was it Ethel? I don't know Ethel's voice, but I don't think so. It could be anyone. Maybe it's the mob. Maybe it's the general's secretary. It scared me to death to hear such a nasty message. Yet, it seems to be the same game as Jean Kennedy's letter because *I'm not having an affair with Bobby*! Someone is trying to make it look like I am!

It's 12305 Fifth Helena Drive. That has been my goodnight mantra lately. As a kid when I couldn't sleep, I memorized the states backward and forward alphabetically. My other trick is to name all the kindnesses in years past, the really obscure, small, authentic moments. Like Anne Bancroft when we were working on *Don't Bother to Knock* saying how well trained I was. Like Lucille Ryman, the talent scout who fed me. Freddy Karger who taught me the pleasures of singing and sex. Whitey—my Dr. Jekyll and Mr. Hyde makeup artist. Better than anyone, he knows Marilyn's look—foreshadowing a sexual explosion—something like that. The transformation from me to Marilyn, like Clark Kent stepping out of the phone booth. I remember the cast allowing me to appear incognito at Martin Beck Theater during the curtain call of *The Teahouse of the*

August Moon so I could get my name at Jim Downey's Restaurant. And Hitchcock, including me alongside Ingrid Bergman and Liz as the best actresses of his lifetime. Remembering kindness is a powerful trick. I mean, you can get a lot of mileage out of a single kind word.

AUGUST 4, 1962

Dear Red,

Tashi arrived early with more plants for the garden. I was already up exercising at eight o'clock. I made my phone calls and drank grapefruit juice and arranged for a Briggs delivery for tonight's dinner with Rafe. I've been pacing around, jumping rope, lifting weights, pondering the strange female voice last night. Mrs. Murray "had to get some work done on her car," she said, before she can pack up and leave Sunday, Monday at the latest. Pat and I hung out by the pool after I chewed her out for sleeping so long—but she forgave me. She's feeling better. We got to work on a pile of scripts. I got a thank-you for my donation to the national Institute for the Protection of Children in Mexico City. That was months ago. Hoover probably turned my donation into proof of my communist politics.

The mail carrier also brought a mystery package—a little stuffed tiger with no name or message attached. Another depressing spook?

Bobby stopped by! He apologized for not returning my calls. He can't risk a phone call—it had to be in person. I went inside for drinks. When I came back to the garden, Pat and Bobby were making out on the chaise lounge!

I tiptoed up to them and whispered like all the world was listening, "So you're the ones having the affair!" I laughed. "Now it's all starting to make sense! I just didn't get it. Everyone is pinning it on me!"

"Sweetie, I apologize!" Pat said. "I was dying to tell you, but Bobby and I made a pact to keep it top secret."

"I guess I'm blind as a bat!" I said. "But tell me, Bobby, do you want your family to think the affair is with me so they don't take it seriously?"

I started to stutter and sob when I told him about last night's phone calls. Bobby calmed me down. Both he and Pat wrapped their arms around me. I grabbed the stuffed tiger and asked him to explain it, since I seem to be the last one to catch on with what's going on. They shushed me, reminding me that if I yell the recording device can pick it up. Bobby tossed it over the fence into the front yard. He said his sister is jumping to conclusions and then asked if I had any dealings with the Mafia recently, and I told him about Giancana at Cal Neva and he put his face in his hands.

"Marilyn, baby, no! I'm so sorry," he whispered. "That bastard!" he said. Then he held his head up high and looked at me. "Marilyn, you're beyond intimidation. Look what you just accomplished with your new contract. I haven't gotten a chance to congratulate you. Way to go. You are an amazing businesswoman on top of all your other talents. I promise. No one will dare make fun of you now. You're getting the respect you deserve."

He cleared his throat and asked a favor—that I destroy all the photographs from Palm Springs and Santa Monica and any letters or notes I have from Jack. Then he asked me again to destroy Red. "Several people want to get their hands on it," he said. "Pillow talk could kill us all, Marilyn."

I nodded. The three of us held each other, our cheeks touching. I laughed, but I felt out of it, like everybody watched the same TV show except me.

I told Bobby I flushed my medicine down the toilet, and he gave me two Nembutal and left to catch a plane back to San Francisco. Pat was next to me on the bed, and I said, "Your affair is the reason I was whisked away to Cal Neva. That's what Frankie said, and I didn't believe him."

She said, "Bobby is the love of my life."

I said, "I'm in shock! I'm happy for you."

When she went into the guest room and shut the door, I put on some Louis Armstrong and took an ice bath. Afterward, I rubbed myself down with Hawaiian oils, a birthday gift from Rafe. I covered my face with a towel and gave my body a twenty-minute nude sunbath treat in the hot sun until I throbbed. It was eerie how I didn't hear any songbirds. I was listening. Maybe Rachel Carson is right about the world falling to pieces.

Red, no one will ever find you. Tashi will make sure. Besides, everyone would be so disappointed if it was ever published—they think my diary is about *them*, but it is all about *me*.

Joe Jr. called to say he broke his engagement. I'm so glad. Not that I didn't like the girl. I mean, she just didn't seem to love him enough. She's all about the suburban house, and car, and bows in her hair, and being married to a famous name bullshit. I told him this gently, because you never know with love—maybe they'll get back together.

Oh, fuck! Is that Dr. G's voice I hear? Mrs. Murray must have let him into the house. I specifically told her not to open the door for anyone except for Rafe, who is coming to dinner. Pat is shouting at Dr. G. He must have woken her up. He's telling her to go home—I hear his every word: "Marilyn is agitated, and Mrs. Murray is going to give her some medication. Just an enema, not an injection. Yes, she is a licensed nurse."

Oh, God damn it! My housekeeper is really a nurse? Back in the vault, Red! I've got to let Pat see I'm fine. I was just in the garden—not even dressed—enjoying a quiet evening.